BURY
the
BISHOP

Kate
Gallison

D1026228

A DELL BOOK

Published by
Dell Publishing
a division of
Bantam Doubleday Dell Publishing Group, Inc.
1540 Broadway
New York, New York 10036

ISBN: 0-440-21854-3

Printed in the United States of America

Published simultaneously in Canada

February 1995

10 9 8 7 6 5 4 3 2

OPM

To Glea Humez

"DON'T TOUCH IT."
THE DETECTIVE GRABBED HER WRIST.

Without touching the paper, she read it out loud:

" 'I saw what you did to the bishop. I thought you might like to make a contribution to my college fund. I'm starting at Harvard next year.' And it's signed Wesley Englebrecht."

"Is there something you want to tell me about this note, Vinnie?"

There was a long silence. Detective Dogg looked completely miserable.

"Am I under arrest?" she said finally.

He appeared to pull himself together, and said, "Maybe you can explain how this got on your desk."

"No," she said. "This office is always locked. Unless I'm here."

"Vinnie, I'll be straight with you. This puts you right back at the top of the list of suspects."

"I can see how that would be so," she said. "But you know, Dave, truly, I didn't kill anybody."

He sighed, and suddenly resumed the granite mask of professionalism, Dave Dogg the cold upholder of law and order. "You might think about getting a lawyer."

"Thank you," she said, for what she wasn't sure. . . .

ACKNOWLEDGMENTS

The author wishes to acknowledge the assistance of Fr. Richard Townley, Barbara Townley, the Ladies' Choir of St. Andrew's Episcopal Church (Lambertville), Barbara Petty of Fisherman's Mark, and Harold Dunn of the New Jersey State Library.

Prayers and services quoted are from *The Book of Common Prayer*.

I

1

Phyllis Wagonner was crying when she walked into Delio's to meet Mother Grey for breakfast.

Mother Grey observed this fact with a certain amount of un-Christlike irritation. Phyllis had relapsed into crying again, and Mother Grey would now have to abandon her plans for a peaceful breakfast of coffee, cranberry muffin, and *The New York Times* and deal with her somehow. For Mother Grey was not only the vicar of St. Bede's Episcopal Church, Fishersville, and thus Phyllis's pastor, she was also Phyllis's therapist. She had been so sure that Phyllis was well that she had discharged her as a client.

But now she saw that it was not to be. On this otherwise pleasant Friday morning in the little river town of Fishersville, the sun shining, the leaves crisply falling, the last birds of summer calling good-bye before departing New Jersey for wherever it was that they went until spring, on this

1

excellent morning, the very morning when Mother Grey and Phyllis had agreed to meet in Delio's to have breakfast together and plan their strategy for the yearly diocesan convention, which was to begin that afternoon, Phyllis was crying again.

That was how they had met. Shortly after the Department of Missions had sent Mother Grey to Fishersville to take over St. Bede's, the phone rang in the little office under the church where she sat riffling through the overdue bills. The caller identified herself in a low, well-modulated voice as Phyllis Wagonner.

"I understand that you take clients for counseling. Could I come and talk to you sometime during the next few days?"

"No problem," said Mother Grey, and there certainly wasn't. A paying client.

Since Mother Grey was new in town, she had no idea just then who Phyllis was, or her family. Wagonner, though, rang a bell. After making a date with the new client, Mother Grey examined the interior of St. Bede's for clues. Sure enough, the name of Wagonner was appended to most of the furnishings.

First she found that the marble baptismal font was carved with a legend indicating that it was the gift of one Cornelius Wagonner. Next there were the eight stained-glass windows inset with labels saying "Donated for the Glory of God and in loving memory of Mary Withers Wagonner." The windows were tall, beautiful things, depicting various saints and angels. From the delicate style of them

Mother Grey guessed they were English, probably installed at the turn of the century, when people in the town still had money and still lavished it on the Episcopal church.

The church records were full of Wagonners being married, baptized, and buried, together with Witherses, van Buskirks, and Smythes, all the way back to 1870, the year the church was built. Here was Phyllis herself, baptized in 1947. No record of her being married, at least not here. The only child of Arthur Wagonner and Prudence Smythe Wagonner. Hmm. She would have been Mary Withers Wagonner's great-granddaughter. Prudence Smythe Wagonner had been buried from St. Bede's in 1988, by Father Ephraim Clentch, Mother Grey's predecessor, and Arthur Wagonner had been transferred out of the parish the following year to a parish in Palm Beach, Florida. The Wagonners were old money, evidently. Mother Grey wondered why she had never seen Phyllis in church.

At breakfast she asked Horace who the Wagonners were.

Twice a week, Mother Grey could afford to go to Delio's and take her breakfast with Horace Burkhardt, the dapper old man of the town. He was there every morning in his threadbare jacket and tie having coffee and a cake cruller, as doughnuts were called in this part of New Jersey, and looking for fun. They enjoyed each other's company; he thought Mother Grey was a cute young thing, and she thought he knew the entire history of the town.

At thirty-five, Mother Grey did not consider herself particularly young. Though she was slim and on the short side, she suffered no man under the age of eighty to call her cute. Not even petite. But Horace was over eighty. And as a source of lore he was invaluable, although he didn't know absolutely everything.

It was Horace who had revealed to Mother Grey that the real name of the people who ran the delicatessen was not Delio but de Leo. The de Leos had been in Fishersville for enough generations (three was what it seemed to take) for their family name to become Anglicized on the lips of the locals into deli-oh, which was how they pronounced it themselves these days. One of the de Leos was married to the granddaughter of Mrs. van Buskirk, the oldest living parishioner at St. Bede's. This explained why Lisa van Buskirk de Leo never came to St. Bede's; she went to the Roman church, St. Joseph the Worker, with her Italian-American in-laws. (The other van Buskirk grandchildren had dispersed to other parishes.)

It was the Wagonners who had built the umbrella factory, Horace explained. "Wagonner's Umbrellas, Mother Vinnie, you must remember them." Mother Grey tried to remember whether she had ever seen a Wagonner's Umbrella. She herself had never owned an umbrella, being given more to raincoats and hats, though in the elephant's foot umbrella stand in the front hall of the house in Washington where Lavinia Grey grew up, her grandmother had kept several. But Wagonner's? No telling.

In any case, the Wagonner's Umbrella was a thing of the past. Empty now, the old factory stood between the river and the canal on March Street. Gone was the dignified sign that used to say "Wagonner Brothers Manufacturing." The multinational conglomerate that bought the business from Phyllis's father had torn it down and replaced it with another, "Pop-o Umbrellas." Mother Grey remembered seeing that sign, or what was left of it, on her morning walks. Boys had used it for slingshot practice. Odd that the company would invest in an expensive neon sign just before closing the factory and firing all those people.

About Phyllis herself, Horace didn't seem to have much to say, except that he remembered her as a little girl, and he noticed that after she grew up and came back from college, she was different. "If you know what I mean," he said. Mother Grey didn't know what he meant. He said, "Well, now she's the town librarian." A good-looking woman. People wondered sometimes why she had never married, but Horace just figured it was because she thought she was too good for the Fishersville men. "That's what happens when you send girls to college," said Horace.

Of course! The librarian. Now Mother Grey recognized the voice. The library was one of the first places she had gone to establish herself in the town. Phyllis Wagonner was that tall librarian who sniffled.

That, as it turned out, was her presenting symptom of emotional distress. She cried all the time. It was becoming a problem. Phyllis dealt with the public on a daily basis; she feared that not all of her patrons believed the stories she told them of summer colds, or winter colds, or allergies. At the first counseling session, when Mother Grey pressed her for the cause of her attacks of weeping (". . . and what are you thinking about, when you find yourself starting to cry?") Phyllis said that random thoughts or stories set her off, ancient memories of drowned kittens or dead relatives, or newspaper accounts of the deaths of children. Thoughts of these things would come to her mind as she went about her daily activities. Then she would start to cry and not be able to stop.

They set a goal for the therapy, which was to be short term: Turn off the waterworks so that Phyllis might get on with her life in some sort of normal way.

They discussed her feelings. Nothing severely unpleasant had happened to Phyllis lately, other than the approach of middle age. Mother Grey suggested that the tears might have come from hormone assaults caused by the change of life. Phyllis took this notion to her gynecologist, who prescribed something.

Several weeks into counseling, though, Phyllis revealed what was really troubling her. Years before, her lover had left her pregnant and gone off to Vietnam. In an effort to reclaim her life from the forces of fate, she had obtained an abortion, legally, in a hospital, so that she could finish school. Now she regretted having done this, with greater and greater bitterness. Even as it was happening, she had wanted to get up off the gurney and run out, she said, but by then they had drugged her, they had X-rayed her, it wasn't possible. Already the baby was ruined within her body.

Too late now to have another child. He (she?) would have been twenty. Phyllis cried for the whole hour at that session.

But the very act of ventilating her story, which had not been exposed to the air since the evil morning when they wheeled her, gowned and shower-capped, into the operating room like a sacrificial offering for the doctors, the very telling of it after all this time seemed to ease her mind afterward. Within weeks the chronic weeping dried up.

It was only after her apparent recovery that Phyllis started coming to church again, perhaps in gratitude, although Mother Grey preferred to think it was from a sincere intention to seek the Lord.

They became friends. They had a number of things in common. They both read a great deal. They both loved baroque music. Phyllis had studied the violin and so was able to accompany Mother Grey's cello. Together with Sheila Dresner, the town veterinarian, who also played violin, they met frequently to play string trios.

Basically the three were good friends, although

Sheila once confided in Mother Grey that she thought Phyllis was awfully brittle, and Phyllis called Sheila "the Yenta" behind her back (whatever that meant), and the Lord alone knew what either of them said about Mother Grey when she wasn't there. The three women had another thing in common besides their music: Their professional services—salvation, erudition, animal health— were perceived by most of the townspeople as useless.

The people of Fishersville by and large were what Lavinia's grandmother would have called ordinary, because she was too well-bred to call them common. (Ordinary people clipped their nails in the living room, combed their hair in the dining room, ate with the wrong fork, if any, and used words like *ain't*.)

They were not looking for library books. Horace's scorn for education (and not only education for women) was shared by most of the townspeople, including, as rumor had it, a number of school board members.

Nor did they have any use for veterinary care. It cost money, and it was never covered by insurance. "Let the old cat die" wasn't just an expression here. After one's job goes, medical treatment for one's pets is not at the top of one's to-do list. Luckily for Sheila, she was married to a stockbroker who commuted to the city every day and brought home big money. They had moved to Fishersville ten years before because they thought it was quaint.

Well, it *was* quaint. Sort of. But Lavinia Grey, along with her fellow purveyors of unappreciated luxuries, lived almost on the fringes of Fishersville society. At the center were the four volunteer fire companies and the rescue squad, because this was the sort of saving that the locals were most urgently in need of. Immediate rescue, from the flames, from the river, from the auto wreck. Spiritual salvation was a bit more iffy.

There were plenty of other churches in town, more prosperous and better attended than St. Bede's: Withers Avenue Presbyterian, Jesus My Light AME, First Baptist, Fishersville Assembly of God, and St. Joseph the Worker. But the folk Mother Grey had come to town to minister to, at least in her own mind, since there were so few practicing Episcopalians, were the common people—sorry, Granny, ordinary people—who didn't go to church and who needed so much help. Alas, it was true that she seldom found them consciously looking for God.

Bishop Everett Wealle himself had explained about the uselessness of Mother Grey's mission to Fishersville the day he told her she was called to be the vicar there. "St. Bede's is functionally dead," the bishop had said to her upon presenting her with this, her first parish. "Take a few months to put its affairs in order and close it down. It's valuable real estate; we can still use its assets to do the Lord's work. Then I'll see that you're assigned to a real parish." A dispiriting interview.

When she saw the false parish up close, Mother

Grey had to agree that it was not in good shape. The parish register revealed that no one had been married, baptized, or confirmed at St. Bede's for years, and even the funerals were becoming more and more infrequent. The church building was rotting. Buckets nestled here and there among the pews to receive rainwater. For her first Sunday services, three frail old women came to hear Mother Grey's maiden sermon and receive Communion. No one else appeared.

But though it might be dying, the parish of St. Bede's was not yet dead, and Mother Grey was vain enough to love it simply because it was her own. Surely St. Bede's could have a place in God's plan other than as brute real estate. The church building was well worth preserving and cherishing. Those parts that were not completely decayed were lovely, the windows, the oaken pews, the brass Communion rail with its design of ivy leaves. If only there were money for repairs.

That so few of the people in the old river town of Fishersville were communicants in the Episcopal Church was by no means a sign to Mother Grey that the church had no mission there. Need was everywhere. Day care, drug and alcohol counseling, shelter for the homeless, programs for the elderly, care for battered women—Fishersville cried out for all of this and more. If only someone cared.

If only the bishop cared. When she mentioned it to him, he chuckled indulgently and accused her of foolish idealism. It made her furious to be patronized, and the worst of it was that people did it all the time because she was so slight and delicate in appearance. On the way to the priesthood she had developed ways of projecting her true personality, mature, stubborn, indomitable, and (she liked to think) somewhat ruthless and hard-bitten. These techniques of posture and voice never worked on the bishop. Verbally and sometimes physically he was always patting her on the head.

She meant to corner him at the diocesan convention this afternoon and take up the cudgels again. St. Bede's and its mission must be supported. Last Sunday there were five people at Holy Eucharist, even without Hester Winkle and Ida Mae Soames, who had gone away to the nursing home the week before. Mother Grey's flock—she actually thought of them sometimes as her flock—was growing.

Lavinia Grey was not by nature a particularly effective pastor, or so she believed. The art of being a good pastor, of leading people out of their troubles and into the truth of Jesus Christ, had to be studied and learned, not unlike psychological counseling. For one thing, her gut-level reaction to people who were sick or in pain was usually one of antipathy. *You impossibly stupid person, how could you keep doing this to yourself?* All of which is not to say that she didn't love her fellow humans; she did; that's why they made her so mad.

She was tempted to feel angry at Phyllis. However great her private pain might be, Phyllis was blessed by God in many ways. At forty-five, she was a handsome woman, in excellent health. She had a profession and a comfortable private income on top of it. Her father was living a healthy, sober, independent life in Palm Beach, where he had retired after the sale of the umbrella factory. No one had abused her as a child, sexually or otherwise. She had never gone hungry; she had always had clothes, shoes, a roof over her head. These things were not true of everyone in Fishersville.

These things were not even true of everyone breakfasting in Delio's at this very moment. The three carpenter's helpers in a cloud of cigarette smoke at the table by the door were regulars at the Alcoholics Anonymous session that met at St. Bede's every Saturday. Not all of them were in successful recovery. The schoolteacher hunched in the corner reading *The New York Times* beat his wife. (The wife came to Mother Grey to complain, but she always went back to him.) The young woman buying a quart of milk for her little daughter had no man at home; her husband was in prison, convicted of molesting the daughter. The man lolling on the doorstep outside had spent the night on the riverbank, drunk again, from the smell of him. According to Horace, he had distinguished himself in Vietnam, but now he had no home. Nearly everyone else in sight had worked for Wagonner Brothers. Some had not found other jobs.

And here came Phyllis with her face all blotched and swollen, the badge of another night of weeping.

Not that it was all that apparent to the untrained eye; Phyllis wasn't sobbing or carrying on in such a way as to cause herself great public embarrassment in front of the scornful eyes of a luncheonette full of her father's former employees. But Mother Grey could see it, and she knew at once that her friend was in pain again, that her parishioner was alienated from God's healing presence, that her client was backsliding.

Now she must respond to this, and before she had her coffee too.

The time before morning coffee was for Mother Grey a time devoid of intellectual activity or distinctions of higher feeling, when she simply selected a mode of behavior from her library of automatic reactions and stuck with it until the caffeine kicked in. Such behaviors seemed to her to come from somewhere in her limbic system or lower brain stem, where they had been stored in childhood or in school.

The Anglo-Saxon Politeness mode, oldest and most deeply ingrained, and coldest, dictated that she pretend not to notice her friend's distress but greet her cordially and make small talk until Phyllis recovered her composure.

The pastoral mode of reaction to Phyllis's tears would be to jump up and comfort her. This would make her worse for a while, and the two women would be standing there hugging and blubbering in the face and eyes of a roomful of men who did not particularly like Phyllis. Bad idea.

Phyllis sat down at the table; Mother Grey

folded her *New York Times* and selected a low-key counselor-type approach. She patted her hand.

"Are you all right?"

"I had another nightmare," Phyllis said.

"Let me get you some coffee. You can tell me all about it after we eat."

2

When breakfast was over, Mother Grey bundled the sniffling Phyllis straight from Delio's to the rectory. They walked; it was only two blocks. Towser made a fuss over Phyllis when they came into Mother Grey's kitchen, but not as enormous a fuss as he made over strangers, since Phyllis was a frequent visitor to the house. That was one of the problems with dogs; they tended to bother one's guests. If his owner still hadn't come forward by the time his leg healed, she would get him obedience training.

At the kitchen table Mother Grey and Phyllis laid into the coffee and engaged in nightmare analysis. Phyllis talked; Mother Grey listened. It was the same nightmare Phyllis always had.

The most frightening thing about this dream was that she carried out unspeakable cruelties in it with no sense of repulsion or guilt. The things she did and said seemed reasonable, even inevitable, the normal way to behave. It was only when she awoke that she saw herself as an ogre, a monster. She couldn't forgive herself.

They explored all this from various angles, hoping for new insights, which didn't come. As usual, Mother Grey offered the forgiveness of the Lord, the Christian counselor's ultimate charm against disabling guilt. As usual, Phyllis maintained that the Lord's view of the matter had nothing to do with it. The more Mother Grey urged the goodness of God and His creation, the sweetness, actually, of life, the more truculent Phyllis became. It was almost as though her misery were a treasured possession she was defending. Mother Grey was beginning to think it might be time for Phyllis to find a psychologist in the city. Certainly she could afford one. She was preparing to put forth this suggestion when Phyllis said, "Never mind, Vinnie, let it go for now. Let's just do what we have to do about the convention."

The diocesan convention took place every year during the first weekend in November. Business was conducted there without which the business of the diocese could not legally go forward for the following year. It was a hotbed of the strange politics of the godly. The budget was voted upon. Officers and committee members were elected. Parishes that had not been able to pay their assessment the previous year were publicly humiliated by having their names announced in a loud and scornful voice by the clerk of the diocese. It was a gathering to be prepared for in every parish by an entire year of prayer, fasting, meditation, and forking over the assessment.

More particularly, the priest and three delegates and their alternates (if any) of every parish were to prepare for a month or so beforehand by reading over the packets of convention materials that came in the mail. The diocesan convention packets this year consisted of three fat manila envelopes of colored paper bearing reports, resolutions, and slates of officers and committeepersons for the coming year. These Mother Grey now produced from a drawer in the kitchen.

Since the parish had managed somehow to pay its yearly assessment, St. Bede's was permitted to cast four ballots, one for the clergy and three for the lay delegates, on every question. They needed to plan beforehand how best to vote. It was up to Mother Grey and Phyllis because Ralph and Mrs. van Buskirk, the other two delegates, had declined to come to this morning's meeting, each for a different reason.

Ralph Voercker, Mother Grey's thirty-year-old altar boy, wasn't coming, he had told her, because he had to go look for a job.

Yes, of course he had to go look for a job. But was he actually out job-hunting? Mother Grey thought not. More likely he was still lolling in bed at the young men's group home. It was a tribute to her influence over him that Ralph managed to get to church every Sunday.

Incredibly, Ralph had been married. Mother Grey couldn't imagine what sort of girl had thought Ralph would make a husband. But after three months his wife had left him, whereupon he suffered a breakdown. And everyone around him suffered as well. Ralph never suffered by himself.

That was how Ralph had come to be a parishioner at St. Bede's. Late one night in February there had been a knock on the rectory door, and there stood—not Ralph, but Officer Jack Kreevitch of the Fishersville Police Department.

"We got a jumper on the wing dam, Mother," he said. "Can you talk to him? It's colder'n hell out there." She got into long underwear, sweaters, and jeans with the speed of a fireman and rode out under Kreevitch's screaming siren to the wing dam. Harsh blue searchlights showed a shivering figure far out on the dam. The entire police force of Fishersville clustered on the bank of the river, all five of them, shouting over the roar of the rapids.

The wing dam was the worst place in the river for drownings. They said there was a hollow under the dam, washed away by years of rushing water, eight feet deep maybe, where even a strong man caught in that undertow might stay submerged for days before rescuers could reach his body. Mother Lavinia Grey marched boldly out.

Ralph stood just out of her reach, in water up to his ankles where it rushed over the dam. Ice formed on his pants cuffs. The current was tremendous. A smaller man would have been swept over.

"Give me your hand," said Mother Grey. "It's too cold to stand out here. You'll hurt your feet."

"I want to die," said Ralph.

"Plenty of time for that later," said Mother Grey. "Come inside and get warm."

"Did they call Alice?"

"Come with me. You can call her yourself."

"I told them to call Alice and tell her I was going to kill myself."

"They couldn't reach her. Come on, you're going to catch cold." The water, sliding away and away under her feet, was making her dizzy.

He stared at her, slack-jawed. "Couldn't reach her?"

"No, dear."

"Shit," he said, and wiped his nose on the back of his hand. " 'Scuse my French."

"Give me your hand." He gave her his hand, not the one he had used on his nose, happily, and came with her quietly, which was good because she really felt that at any moment she was going to lose her balance, fall into the black icy water, and disappear under the dam.

After she went with him in the police car to Hunterdon Medical Center, after she sat with him for hours while he waited to be admitted to the mental ward, after she visited him once a day for the month that it took him to get his head together, after she found him a bed in the local halfway house for disturbed young men and got him a job, Ralph Voercker was her slave.

Alice never did turn up. She had made good her

escape. Papers came from a lawyer in Reno, causing Ralph to go crazy again for a little while, but another week in the medical center put him back on track. The fact that he followed Mother Grey around all the time was gratifying, sort of, but it would have been even nicer if he got himself all the way together and began to lead a normal life.

Sometimes he said he wanted to be a minister. He was better at being a ministry; a minister normally has a little something on the ball. But Ralph was actually pretty good as an altar boy, and if nothing terrible happened, he would pass for a convention delegate in a dim light.

It had taken her a week to talk him into it.

Even as she was telling him how much they needed him, how useful he would be, Mother Grey wondered about it herself. He was not all that presentable in public. If it weren't for the necessity for every respectable parish priest in the Diocese of New Jersey to show up at the diocesan convention accompanied by three lay bodies, she would have let Ralph stay home and read his Marvel comics. But she really, really needed him. In these precarious times it was crucial to give the impression of a thriving, growing parish.

Her clinching argument was a pitch about the welfare of St. Bede's itself, how they needed to present a full complement of delegates in order to impress the bishop, who, as they all knew, would seize upon any excuse to close St. Bede's. ("So, Mother Grey! I see you could only find two lay delegates to bring to convention. Too bad for St. Bede's.")

"If there were anyone else, Ralph, I wouldn't ask you to do it," she said, and that was the truest thing she said to him. At last Ralph agreed to come. He refused, however, to attend the war council that was to be held beforehand.

"You tell me how to vote, Mother Vinnie," he said. "You tell me what to do." She promised to fill him in on the issues after the morning meeting, during the half-hour car ride to Trenton. No point in forcing him to read all these reports. It would be after Epiphany by the time he finished.

As for Mrs. van Buskirk, the reason she wouldn't come to the meeting was that at the age of ninety-two she was enjoying some kind of adolescent rebellion.

For the first time in her long years of convention-going, Delight van Buskirk had decided to vote her own mind. She did not want to have her mind muddled by going over the convention materials beforehand with Phyllis and Mother Grey. This year, she said, Effie Bingley's boy was running again for a position on the powerful Department of Missions, and old Father Clentch was no longer around to bully her out of voting for him.

Father Bingley, the rector of St. Dinarius, was no longer a boy and in Mother Grey's private opinion was eminently unfit for a position on the Department of Missions. For one thing, he gave every evidence of profound stupidity; for another, he was a right-wing nut; and for a third, the Department of Missions had direct jurisdiction over all the mission churches and thus over St. Bede's.

Mother Grey in all innocence had asked Mrs. van Buskirk after church on Sunday whether she would like a ride to the preconvention meeting at the rectory. "No thank you, dear," the old lady said. "I think I'll let you hold that one without me. I've already read everything in my convention packet." Her plan, as Mother Grey understood it, was to fill the important committee posts with the children and grandnephews, be they never so feebleminded, of her old girlfriends; on the important social questions she meant to vote her whims, since there was no longer a male priest at St. Bede's to tell her what to do. She as much as declared these intentions to Mother Grey (not the feebleminded part, of course). What she said was, "It's not that I don't respect you, dear. Please don't think that. I'm very glad to have you here at St. Bede's. It's just that now, at last, I feel perfectly free to vote as I wish."

"But we need your input," Mother Grey begged; the old lady only smiled archly, as though suspecting some sort of trap. Evidently Father Clentch had been given to bullying his delegates.

So Mother Grey and Phyllis were forced to make all the important decisions by themselves.

"Have you ever been to this thing before?" Phyllis asked. "I know you weren't ordained until last December."

"Once, two years ago," said Mother Grey, "when I was still a deacon."

22

"What was it like?"

"I found it entertaining. The most interesting thing, I thought, was to see the diversity of the people in the Diocese of New Jersey who called themselves Episcopalians. It's nothing like the old days, when most of us were middle-class WASPs."

"I can hardly wait," said Phyllis, and Mother Grey realized that for Phyllis the ethnic diversity of the convention would be its least gratifying aspect. Phyllis was something of a bigot. Well, perhaps not a bigot; more of an elitist. Or no, not an elitist either. Actually, Phyllis hated everybody.

The matters to be voted upon were significant this year. There was the Unified Budget, a change in the bookkeeping and budget projection that would radically affect diocesan financing. The vote was expected to result in a revision of canon law so that there would be one budget instead of two.

Phyllis wanted to know why there were two budgets to begin with. "Is the diocese keeping the proverbial two sets of books?"

"No, no," said Mother Grey, "but there are two budgets. As nearly as I can figure out, one budget is a list of all the projects and expenses that the parishes feel divinely inspired to subsidize, and the other is a detailed projection of what the bishop feels divinely inspired to spend."

"And for some reason the parishes want these two budgets to become one."

"Yes, the parishes feel that they would have

more control that way over where their money goes."

"Are you saying the bishop is spending money that the parishes don't want to give him?"

"The parishes don't *want* to give him anything. But they *have* to give him a certain amount to run the diocese, and they're *supposed* to give him a certain other amount on top of that, to support the national Church, to help foreign missions, and all the rest of it."

"Voluntarily."

"Yes, voluntarily. We are a church after all, Phyllis. This isn't the government or the Cosa Nostra. And you have to remember that the whole point of the Episcopal Church is that we have bishops whose authority can be traced back to Peter. The very word *Episcopal* means having to do with bishops. Without our bishops we wouldn't be who we are."

"What if we broke away and declared ourselves independent?"

"Phyllis!"

"Just as a hypothetical question."

"The diocese would take away the church, the roof over my head, and just about everything we have here. The courts say they own it all."

"It's been tried, then."

"What is this, Phyllis? I thought you wanted to come to this convention. What do you have against the bishop?"

"Against the bishop!" said Phyllis. "Why, nothing. So tell me what else goes on this afternoon."

24

"The other thing they're doing this year is the racial audit."

"Which is what?"

"It's a sort of litmus test for political correctness that came out of the general convention in Phoenix last year."

"Should we study for it?" said Phyllis.

"No, it's more of a pop quiz."

"What's it for?" said Phyllis. "Will the Department of Missions cut off our funds if we fail it?"

"I think it's an exercise in introspection, or an anonymous survey. Probably we won't even be expected to put our names on the answer sheet," said Mother Grey. Or so she hoped. If one-fifth of Mother's Grey's congregation, namely Phyllis, were unmasked as a drooling racist, what would the Department of Missions have to say about it? She could hear the bishop: *I'm sorry, Mother Grey, but your parish is politically incorrect. We're going to be forced to close you down.*

"Let's eat lunch," she said. They ate lunch, a desultory meal of canned soup and soda crackers. They made their more or less final decisions. The Unified Budget was to be approved. Father Bingley was not suitable for the Department of Missions. About a number of other issues and candidates they were lukewarm.

When their deliberations were finished, they were ready to load the convention materials into the trunk of Mother Grey's car, together with Mother Grey's vestments—the clergy would be vesting for Holy Eucharist in the cathedral—and a stack of tourist brochures from the Fishersville Chamber of Commerce, featuring a nice photo of St. Bede's on the third page.

"We'll give these out to everybody," said Mother Grey. "It's important for people to know that St. Bede's is a presence in the town."

They drove down the street to the group home to get Ralph, and then up the hill to the old farmhouse where Mrs. van Buskirk lived, surrounded now by a hideous development of condos. Ralph and Mrs. van Buskirk had no transportation of their own from Fishersville to Trenton. It was just as well, in Ralph's case. If he had his own car, he would have weaseled out of the four o'clock Holy Eucharist services in the cathedral, promising to meet them later, and after that it would have been a gamble whether he would show up at the War Memorial Auditorium for dinner and the business meeting.

Mrs. van Buskirk and Ralph sat in the back. The old lady rambled on about the eminent fitness and competence of Effie Bingley's son. In Mother Grey's estimation, Father Bingley's most suitable position would be as chaplain of a golf course in someplace like Parsippany. *Father Bingley is as close to a low-grade moron as anyone I have ever seen in the priesthood. He will achieve a position on the Department of Missions over my dead body*, thought Mother Grey, but she said, "My, yes, Mrs. Bingley must be very proud." They arrived in time to find a parking place in the cathedral lot.

As she collected the bag with her vestments and

took her leave of Phyllis and the other lay delegates, Mother Grey scanned her friend's face for
signs of any recurrence of the morning's hysterics.
Phyllis appeared to have herself well in hand. It
was Ralph who was suddenly anxious: "Where are
you going, Mother Vinnie?"

"The clergy are vesting for this," she explained
to him. "I have to go downstairs and get ready.
We'll be sitting on the gospel side, and you three
will sit with the rest of the laity. I'll meet you after
Mass."

Mrs. van Buskirk shuddered, and Mother Grey
remembered too late how uncomfortable it made
her when Mother Grey used the word *Mass;* the
term was popish, the old lady always insisted, too
High Church. Ecumenism was going to be a tough
sell in Fishersville.

Phyllis took Ralph by the arm. "We sit on the
groom's side," she said. "Mother Vinnie sits on the
bride's side. Come on with us, Ralph." He was still
rolling his eyes in panic as Phyllis and Mrs. van
Buskirk led him around to the front.

In the cathedral undercroft, where vesting was
to take place, Mother Grey found a spot at one of
the long tables next to an old friend. It was Deacon
Deedee Gilchrist, her roommate from her last year
at seminary. They hugged each other in greeting.
Deedee asked how things were at St. Bede's in the
Weeds.

As they struggled into their vestments, Mother
Grey told Deedee a little of how things were at St.
Bede's. "Doesn't look like I'll be the rector any-

time soon," she said. To be a rector in the American Episcopal Church, one had to be in charge of an independent parish, one that supported itself. A mere vicar, on the other hand, was the priest of a mission church that had to accept financial assistance and administrative instruction from the onerous Department of Missions. St. Bede's was officially classified as an incorporated mission.

Deedee herself was not yet ordained to the priesthood. She was serving a trial period at Holy Assumption in Ocean Prospect, where the rector was the popular Canon Arthur Spelving. Spelving was a rector, for Holy Assumption supported itself nicely.

Deedee was statistically typical of the seminary graduates that year in that she was female and forty-three years old. Late vocation. Her children were grown, her husband had run off with some tootsie from his office, so she had turned to the Lord.

Many were the nights they had sat up playing whist, discussing theology, or trading stories about their lives in the world. The year they shared the apartment was remarkable not only for the charm of Deedee's company but also for the late-night telephone calls from Deedee's ex-husband, who would get drunk and call her up to whine about the way the tootsie was treating him. Lavinia Grey's own husband had died; she still mourned him, but at least she didn't have to deal with telephone calls from him. Somehow Deedee dealt with these onslaughts with grace and resilience.

"How do you like working with Arthur Spelving?" Mother Grey asked.

"Very much," said Deedee. "He's an amazing man. I wouldn't be at all surprised if he were to become our next bishop." Bishop! She hadn't thought about it, but it was true that Bishop Wealle could be expected to think about retiring sometime in the next two or three years. Mother Grey would be surprised, though, if the next one were Arthur Spelving, since the very qualities that so endeared Canon Spelving to the younger priests— his activism, his aggressive programs of outreach, his impatience with the notion that suffering was to be stoically endured in this life so that rewards could be enjoyed in the next, when the pie was dished up in the sky—were considered radical by certain factions in the Diocese of New Jersey. Then there were his much-photographed appearances in soup kitchens and cardboard shanty-towns, his lobbying and picketing activities in Trenton and Washington, and his books, three of them, each more embarrassing to the power structure than the one before. Bishop? Unlikely. But then, you never knew.

It would be wonderful, though, if he were the bishop, Mother Grey thought. Quite apart from the fact that they were old friends, he would be much easier than Everett Wealle to convince of the value of St. Bede's. But alas, it was Everett Wealle she was forced to deal with. "Have you seen Bishop Wealle? I need to talk to him as soon as possible."

"Too late," came Deedee's voice from the depths of her half-donned vestments. "Catch him after we dress."

Alas, no opportunity presented itself as the clergy vested, processed, sang, prayed, and heard Bishop Wealle ask the Lord to bless their coming deliberations. Nor yet after the Mass was over. She saw the bishop leave and made a dive toward the door after him, but the wretched Father Bingley was blocking the exit. When Mother Grey asked whether he knew which way the bishop had gone, he merely raised his eyebrows and shook his head.

So Mother Grey went to collect her delegates. She found them sightseeing in the cathedral. They were examining one of the ornate windows, a stained-glass depiction of Saint Hilda of Whitby.

Saint Hilda presented an arresting image; dressed in nun's garb, haloed in red, she carried what appeared to be a crozier—the ornate shepherd's crook symbolic of the office of bishop—in her left hand. Her right hand was upraised to admonish a dais full of dignitaries, men clothed as kings and rich clerics. The dignitaries appeared to stare at one another in alarm. Two white swans—geese? ducks?—flew over their heads. Mother Grey found a personal message in this spectacle in stained glass. She saw herself, explaining the plight of St. Bede's to the bishop and the Department of Missions.

"I like this," said Phyllis. "But who was Saint

Hilda of Whitby? She seems to be telling all these men where to get off."

"Yes, doesn't she? But I've no idea who she was," Mother Grey confessed. "I'll have to look it up." Who, indeed? Had some holy icon of feminism found its way into Trinity Cathedral? And what was the significance of the ducks?

Mother Grey imagined her own self gripping a crozier, perhaps wagging the finger of rebuke at a grandstand full of churchmen. *Now see here, Everett*, she rehearsed.

3

Back in the car, Delight van Buskirk refused to let Mother Grey follow the herd to the John Fitch Expressway. "Don't be silly, dear," she said. "Just go straight up West State Street and turn right at Willow. They're only going that way because they're afraid of getting lost in the city."

Mother Grey drove the few blocks eastward to the War Memorial Auditorium without incident. She had grown up in a city, none other than Washington, D.C., and she wasn't afraid of cities, only of getting lost. Since they arrived early, they secured a good parking place behind the statehouse, right across the street from the War Memorial Auditorium.

Pillared, porticoed, and lit by spotlights, the War Memorial had an air of grandeur that recalled the public architecture of Washington itself. As Mother Grey and her companions climbed the white marble steps, going slowly for the sake of

Delight van Buskirk, they looked back over their shoulders to see the cars of the other out-of-towners come straggling in off the Fitchway. "I told you so," said the old lady, shaking her cane. "We'll be the first ones to dinner."

They found groups of smokers clustered here and there on the windy portico. It was an interesting space, architecturally. Embedded in the marble walls were bronze plaques bearing the homely faces of local industrialists, important men of the days when Trenton had had industry. Presumably they had built the hall. "What's this? The Court of Capitalists?" said Phyllis.

"Now, Phyllis, don't sneer at capitalism," said Mrs. van Buskirk. "Capitalism made our country what it is today."

Mother Grey couldn't help laughing, at Phyllis mostly. "Radical politics, Phyllis?" she said.

"You laugh," said Phyllis. "But I used to march in those protest rallies, with my long hair and love beads." Mother Grey tried to picture it. Good heavens, perhaps Phyllis really did want to secede from the diocese.

They stepped inside out of the wind. As they stood in line waiting to register and collect their tickets for dinner, Father Rupert Bingley appeared, his bald head glittering. The very sight of him brought the blood of rage to her face.

Mother Grey had prayed about it, and she felt it as a spiritual failure, but she could never bring herself to forgive Father Bingley for their first encounter. Two days after she moved into St. Bede's rectory, he had driven over from his parish in the wealthy community of Rolling Hills to pay her a call. He came, he said, to offer to take over her parishioners when she closed St. Bede's. "We have our own minivan," he said. "We can call for them at their homes and bus them to St. Dinarius. It's only twenty minutes away."

She refused his offer with cold politeness, assuring him that she had rather hoped to keep St. Bede's open for a while. "I feel there is much to be done here," she said. After he left, she brooded over his visit and became furious. She had been furious ever since.

Delight van Buskirk, knowing nothing of this, greeted him happily. "Rupert, dear, how nice to see you. And how is your dear mother?"

"Mother is not as well as she might be," said Bingley. "Her knees. She said to give you her best regards, Mrs. van Buskirk."

"I must say that Bishop Wealle is looking well this evening."

"Looking well, yes. But I might point out that His Grace isn't wearing it," Bingley said darkly, and glided away into the crowd.

"Not wearing what?" said Phyllis. "Or aren't we supposed to ask?"

"His collar," said Mother Grey.

"Not wearing his clerical collar!" cried Mrs. van Buskirk. "Surely we would have noticed."

"No, the orthopedic one. Rumor has it that his doctors—" Then suddenly she found herself at the head of the line for registration. Between registering, collecting their credentials and dinner tickets, and shepherding the St. Bede's delegation to the banquet room, they were standing in line again, this time for their dinner, before she was able to resume the story of the bishop's collar.

It seemed that the bishop suffered from a degenerative disease of the bones in his neck, or so went the rumor. This unfortunate condition threatened to cause neurological damage unless he wore an orthopedic collar.

The story was that his doctors had ordered him to wear the collar at all times, on pain of severe injury at the slightest jolt. "But he won't wear it to things like this convention because he feels it spoils his dignified image."

"His image," said Delight van Buskirk. "Oh, yes, he's vain. My dears, do you know he waxes his mustache?"

"No," said Phyllis.

"What makes you think so?" Mother Grey said in spite of herself. *I should change the subject*, she thought. *This is very wicked.*

"I know a waxed mustache when I see one," said Mrs. van Buskirk. "They were all the rage when I was a girl."

Ralph smiled, not at the idea of Mrs. van Buskirk's girlhood experience with waxy mustaches, but rather at the sight of the food. "Roast beef," he said. "Excellent." They held their plates out while serving persons heaped them with dinner. They found seats at one of the long tables among the delegates of three other parishes.

Mother Grey applied herself diligently to her meal. Anything that was cooked by someone else was ambrosia to her. While Phyllis began to talk up St. Bede's and hand out the Chamber of Commerce brochures, Ralph went back to the steam table for seconds and thirds.

For dessert the caterers had set every table with plates of delicious little cream puffs dusted with powdered sugar; every table, that is, except the next table over, where Mother Grey could hear the delegation from St. Dinarius complaining of a shortage of desserts. Too bad for Father Bingley; he liked his desserts, as everyone could see from his girth.

In the hallway after dinner, Mrs. van Buskirk denounced their behavior. "Imagine those greedy people from St. Dinarius," Mrs. van Buskirk muttered. "Making a scene over the cream puffs. I thought there were plenty, didn't you?"

"I thought so, yes," said Mother Grey, as she glanced around for the bishop.

"Certainly," said Phyllis.

"Mmf," said Ralph, wiping powdered sugar off his hands and onto his shirt.

Mother Grey's goals for this convention were few; first, she needed to get the bishop in private and pitch the future of St. Bede's to him; second, she needed to impress everybody there with how well the parish was doing generally; and third, she needed to get Ralph in and out without a major contretemps. So far, so good, if only she could find the bishop. Except of course for the suspicious lump in the front of Ralph's shirt, which even now seemed to be oozing cream filling.

Suddenly she felt a clap on the shoulder, and the warm arm of Canon Arthur Spelving. "How are you, Vinnie?" he said.

The arm of Canon Spelving was not a fatherly arm, nor yet the arm of friendship, really, but more of a political arm. Canon Spelving's embraces were meant to include one as a fellow conspirator in his aims and designs. Knowing her liberal leanings, he had come for Mother Grey's vote on his proposed amendment to the Unified Budget.

Mother Grey introduced her delegates. Phyllis was radiant—she could be so, on occasion—and Delight van Buskirk smiled at him and gave him a whole handful of Chamber of Commerce brochures.

"Father Spelving," muttered Ralph, and thrust forth his hamlike hand to grasp that of the canon. A cloud of powdered sugar erupted from the place where their palms met.

Oblivious to the spreading trail of white, Canon Spelving clasped Mother Grey again by the shoulder of her dark gray suit and murmured, "We need to talk later." In case she wanted to speak in support of his amendment, he said, he was willing to explain it in detail.

"What a charming man. Is he running for anything?" said Phyllis, as Canon Spelving disappeared at a brisk athletic trot into the auditorium.

"Bishop, I think," said Mother Grey. They fol-

lowed him inside. The auditorium was dimly lit
and cavernous. In the front, the black stage was
framed by swags of gold-fringed red velvet.
Against the black backdrop a twenty-foot banner
hung down, the banner of the diocese, white with
stylized crosses of blue and red.

The delegation from St. Bede's found seats and
settled themselves. Ralph began openly gobbling
his ill-gotten cream puffs, getting powdered sugar
all over the chair arms. Mrs. van Buskirk pointed
out to everyone who would listen that the diocesan
banner was full of creases. "I'd like to take an iron
to it," she said. She would have done a good job
too. There were no uncalled-for wrinkles in the
linens of St. Bede's.

Mother Grey gazed at the ceiling, in itself a work
of art, and at the stage. Beside the banner was a
large arrangement of flowers, a spray of gladiolus,
carnations, and occasional blood-colored lilies.
Chatting among themselves at a table on the apron
below the main stage sat the bishop, the chancellor, and Archdeacon Wilfred de Loeb Megrim,
president of the Standing Committee and the
bishop's right-hand man. Floor-length red draperies on the front of the table hid their feet—a
shame, Mother Grey thought. You could tell a lot
about what people were thinking by observing
their feet. The chancellor and the archdeacon
wore gray suits, almost like old-time Russian bu-
reaucrats; the bishop was dressed in the purple
cassock of his office. Sure enough, he wasn't wearing his orthopedic collar.

Father Bingley came out of the wings and sidled up to the archdeacon, smiling. They exchanged words, evidently of a cordial nature, and Megrim let out an audible guffaw. *Enjoying the ear of the archdeacon, are we, Bingley?* Politics. How Mother Grey hated politics. Then, moments before the opening gavel, down the aisle came Canon Spelving, putting his warm arm around everyone in sight, distributing propaganda for his proposed amendment. He was followed by three of the convention pages, each with a stack of papers, raspberry, goldenrod, and blue. As a fresh-faced young page handed her some of them to pass down the row, Mother Grey found herself entertaining envious thoughts of Holy Assumption's wealth of stationery. It must be nice to have something to protect from the rapacities of the diocese. She thought of having a prosperous church, having a copier. One could do a lot with good office equipment, a copier, a computer, maybe even a fax machine.

After the roll call and the reports of a number of committees came the first ballot. There were only two clergypersons running for the Standing Committee, and Rupert Bingley's name was listed first. This was bad. People who didn't know him might vote for him.

While they were counting ballots, a youth from the Diocesan Youth Ministry by the name of Wesley Englebrecht got up and gave a speech about how he had spent two weeks that summer at a mission in Zambia. Something about the boy's face reminded her of Stephen. He was about the age Stephen had been when they met. Had he really been dead for seven years?

She tried to concentrate on what the boy was saying. Nothing in his talk told what he might have seen or done in Zambia, whom he might have met, what their concerns might have been. He spoke only of himself and how much he had grown; indeed, he was as self-absorbed as Ralph. Probably he would include a copy of this speech with every college application. It would perhaps impress the admissions staff. The convention was so pleased to see a young person active in the church that they gave him a standing ovation. After that, said the agenda, it was time for the first report of the Balloting Committee.

Ralph polished off a cream puff, wiped his hands on his pants with a flourish, and began to paw through his convention materials. "Geez, Mother!" he said. "There's more ballots in here! How many times are we going to have to vote?"

"That will depend on how many ballots it takes for the candidates to get a majority of the votes. Sometimes it takes four or five ballots," she told him. The chairman of the Balloting Committee came to the podium then, cleared his throat, and announced that Rupert Bingley had been elected to the Department of Missions on the first ballot.

Everyone clapped. Delight van Buskirk cheered. Mother Grey thought she was going to faint. The bishop declared a short recess and left the stage.

Mother Grey realized, suddenly, that this was probably her last shot at making her pitch for St.

Bede's. Once Bingley and his allies got a firm hold on the ear of the bishop, the mission of St. Bede's would be dog meat. She sprang from her seat and rushed out after him.

Members of the Registration Committee were still manning the tables in front, waiting for stragglers. "Did you see Bishop Wealle come this way?" Mother Grey asked them.

"He went down the stairs," said one of the women, so she went galloping after him, realizing only after she reached the lower-level lobby that the bishop had gone to the men's.

Mortified, even with no one there to see, Mother Grey sought the ladies' room. There she could lurk for a reasonable length of time before casually stepping out and accosting the bishop. It was in her mind also to touch up her face, much in the manner of a cat who washes itself when embarrassed.

A sign over the door marked the ladies' room, a little old-timey lighted silhouette of a lady seated at a dressing table powdering her nose. Mother Grey went inside and set to work with comb and lipstick.

Rupert Bingley left the auditorium in a kind of triumphal progress, shaking hands, having his back slapped, gracefully accepting the admiration and good wishes of his colleagues and parishioners. At last, a place on the powerful Department of Missions!

First thing he would do after they swore him in

was to see about promoting the long-sought merger between St. Dinarius and St. Bede's of Fishersville. Keeping St. Bede's open was a ridiculous waste of scarce resources; there were hardly enough Episcopalians in Fishersville to keep Mother Grey in altar candles. Fortunately, the archdeacon was one hundred percent behind him on this one, and if only they could secure the cooperation of Bishop Wealle, then St. Bede's was his. Those windows would look splendid at St. Dinarius; Father Bingley had already lined up a craftsman who could do the job. The brass altar rail would be a magnificent addition to his chancel. The leaky roof could stay where it was.

As for Mother Grey, she could surely find herself another assignment somewhere. Or get herself to a nunnery. Women had no business in the priesthood anyway. Our Lord's disciples were men, every one of them. *When I can have babies,* he thought, *then women should be priests.* Women priests. What an idea. Priests were not women. Did these driveling feminists think the Church could have been mistaken on this issue for two thousand years?

He needed to talk to the bishop. Now, while his star was at its zenith. They said he had gone to answer a call of nature. There were three men's rooms in the War Memorial building that Rupert Bingley knew of, one downstairs, one upstairs, and one at the back of the auditorium near the stage. Bishop Wealle had been seen heading for the front of the hall, so he must be either down-stairs or upstairs.

It never occurred to him to ask the ladies behind the desk which way the bishop had gone. Taking directions from ladies was not something that Father Rupert Bingley ordinarily did. He simply plunged toward the first staircase he noticed, which headed downward.

He all but collided with a young fellow who was rushing up the other way. It was that boy who had given the speech. How good it was to see a member of the faithful under forty years old. Wesley Englebrecht, that was his name. Father Bingley was very good with names. It was one of the secrets of his success.

"Excuse me, Wesley, but I need to talk to the bishop. Do you suppose I'll find him down there?"

"Talk to the bishop? Down there? I don't think so, sir," said the youth, with a wild look over his shoulder.

So Father Bingley turned and headed upstairs. It was a long time before he thought to ask himself why young Englebrecht was in such a state of agitation.

4

As Mother Grey touched up her lipstick, she found herself working against a vague apprehension that to fix one's face was an unpriestly activity.

Was it sinful vanity for an Episcopal priest to paint her face? They had not addressed the question in seminary. Certainly there were male priests who were vain. The old priest who had preceded Mother Grey as the vicar of St. Bede's, Fishersville, had worn a toupee, it was said. Not a very good one, either; St. Bede's was much too poor a parish to support a great luxuriance of false hair. Then there was Bishop Wealle himself, who for nothing but vanity refused to wear his orthopedic collar. Luckily for Mother Grey, she did not have to support anyone other than her frugal self on her salary from St. Bede's. Thus if she chose to commit vanity by painting her face, she could occasionally find the money for the very best paint. She bought the stuff in department stores and paid dearly for it, but whether or not to actually wear it was one of the trivial moral struggles that she indulged in sometimes to take her mind off real trouble, such as the difficulties at St. Bede's.

Perhaps that had been the reason for Father Clentch's distressing hairpiece. Maybe he wore it in order to appear sufficiently vital and full of pep —virile, if you will—to merit diocesan assistance for St. Bede's. Maybe he wasn't vain at all. With that thought in mind, Lavinia Grey began to apply her lipstick. The effect she was after was one of radiant health and competence.

Some days Mother Grey did fine without lipstick. At thirty-five, she looked as good as she ever had. Good bones. Classic haircut. But the thought of what the bishop might say to her made her feel pale.

Armored at last with a greasy layer of Rose of Picardy (enriched with luscious emollients), Mother Gray went forth into the lower-level lobby to do battle. The War Memorial Auditorium reminded her of St. Bede's a little; the original design of the place was breathtakingly beautiful in its way, but years without upkeep had done their dismal work. One could imagine the lobby the way it had been fifty years ago, packed with the cream of Trenton society besieging the cloakroom for their furs and opera capes. Now there was no one there at all.

Maybe the bishop was still in the men's room. To kill time, Mother Grey bent to take a drink from a fountain, a lovely piece of tilework where ceramic angelfish blew yellow bubbles in an azure sea. The water was cold and fresh. A pair of gold-rimmed spectacles rested behind the fountain's blue lip.

How odd. She picked them up, meaning to dry them on her handkerchief and turn them in later to the lost and found. But when she drew the handkerchief out of her pocket, the lipstick came with it, fell to the floor, and rolled underneath the cloakroom doors.

They were Dutch doors, and though the top half seemed securely locked, the bottom doors gave inward with pressure. She ducked under the top and went in. Spring-loaded, the bottom doors swung shut behind her. It was perfectly dark.

Her foot came down on something soft and fleshy with bones in it, rather like a dead rat. Mother Grey knew the feel of dead rats underfoot from recent encounters in the undercroft of St. Bede's.

There didn't seem to be a light switch. She held the door open far enough to admit a wedge of light from the lobby, hoping to spot the gold lipstick case without having to look at the dead rat. The glazed eyes and repulsive yellow teeth of the one in St. Bede's undercroft still haunted her.

No lipstick in sight. She pushed against the door spring. The wedge of light widened, and there it was, nestled in the folds of a spill of purple gabardine. What Mother Grey saw next was much more terrible than any dead rat. She had found the bishop at last, but it was too late to get his attention.

Kate Gallison

Don't scream, Mother Grey told herself. *Priests don't scream. It's unseemly.* Being careful not to make a scene of any kind, she walked back up the stairs—polished marble, she found time to notice, brown and green, or maybe it was granite, the steps looked like new tombstones—found Archdeacon Megrim, the current president of the Standing Committee, and calmly reported that the bishop had died somehow, and that his body was lying on the floor of the cloakroom of the lower lobby. For a woman in the grip of a violent case of nerves, she thought she did rather well.

How close she was to the edge of nervous hysteria became apparent when a plainclothes officer the color and shape of a fireplug invited her to step into a small office so that he could ask her, as he said, a few questions, and she had to stifle an impulse to laugh in his face. For his credentials revealed that the man rejoiced in the name of David Dogg.

Rejoiced in the name. This archaic expression always struck Mother Grey as funny, fraught as it was with ambiguities. Did the detective pretend to be David Dogg while rejoicing? But no, that would be to rejoice under the name. Did he invoke the name of Dogg while rejoicing? Hallelujah, by Dogg! he cried. The contemplation of this image brought a giggle bubbling to her lips. *I'm losing it*, she thought. Fighting the urge to cry and scream had rotted her mind.

And then she noticed the detective's eye on her. There was nothing doglike about the look in them, nothing at all. *Detective David Dogg thinks I murdered the bishop.*

She returned his gaze levelly, projecting a guiltless and cooperative spirit, as befitted the vicar of St. Bede's. Later there would be time for hysterics.

"If you'll just sit down here, sister, I won't take up very much of your time," said Detective Dogg. "There are a few small things we need to clear up." Another man stood in the shadows, tall, silent, dark, taking notes.

"I'm not a nun," said Mother Grey. "I'm a priest. Please don't call me sister."

He said, "When you found the bishop's body, what did you do?"

"I immediately notified Archdeacon Megrim, and then I called the police."

"Why him first?"

"Canon law," she said. "The president of the Standing Committee must be told immediately of the death of a sitting bishop. Bishop Wealle is—was—a sitting bishop."

"I see."

"And we are in convention, so it's even more important." He was looking at her as if she were raving. Surely what she was saying made sense—?

"Right," he said. "But you didn't scream, or like that. You just went straight to Archdeacon Megrim."

Was it strange that she hadn't screamed? "This is not to say that I wasn't horrified." The bishop's twisted dead face, his hand under her foot. Nightmares.

"Sorry, Reverend, but you just seem awfully cool for somebody who just stepped on a murder victim."

Murder? Unthinkable. "I did no such thing."

"No? I thought you said . . ."

"Bishop Wealle is hardly a murder victim." She told him all about the weakness in the bishop's vertebrae, and the collar he was supposed to wear. Everybody knew about the collar. "Ask his doctor. The bishop's death was clearly accidental." Without the special collar to protect his neck, he had broken it, apparently by catching the heavy chain of his cross on the leg of a folding table stored in the cloakroom. "I'm sure you agree that was what happened." But Mother Grey's legendary powers of persuasion had apparently deserted her. Detective Dogg refused to buy her theory.

"What would Bishop Wealle be doing crawling around on the floor of the cloakroom in the dark?" Dogg asked.

"Perhaps he dropped something," said Mother Grey. "Maybe he dropped a pen. No doubt you'll find whatever it was after they move his body. And my lipstick too."

"Could you tell me what that is on your coat?"

Startled, she looked at her suit jacket and saw two distressing white streaks across the gray flannel. She must have got too close to Ralph. "Powdered sugar," she said. "From our dessert." Actually it was from Ralph. No need to mention it. Or really, it was Father Bingley's dessert. Good heavens, could Ralph get in trouble with the police for stealing cream puffs?

"Dessert," the policeman said, in a carefully neutral tone of voice. The man in the shadows was scribbling furiously. "I see. Now, let's just go over this again, if you don't mind. You say you dropped your . . . lipstick?" They went over it all again. He seemed to have trouble with the idea of a priest wearing lipstick. At some point he started calling her sister again, and she had to tell him again that she wasn't a nun.

She wished she were back in Fishersville, where the police all understood what a parish priest was and called her Mother Vinnie. Since her success with Ralph Voercker the Fishersville police called her for all the suicide attempts. When St. Bede's or the rectory was broken into, she called them. It was a relationship of mutual trust and respect, not the way it was with this person, who behaved as though she might have something to hide, who behaved, in fact, the way a policeman would ordinarily behave toward a woman of God who had just managed somehow to kill her bishop.

At last the interrogation or whatever it was was over. Mother Grey yearned for the solitude of the rectory. *I'm going home now*, she thought, *and when I get there, I'm going to say my prayers and have a good cry.* Though a priest would never scream, it was okay for a priest to cry. Detective Dogg gave her his card and said to call him if she thought of anything else.

Mother Grey left the office with as much dignity

as she could. She did not wish to appear to be fleeing, although that was how she felt. If no one had been watching she would have run the whole way to the auditorium, in high heels and everything, grabbed her delegates, and forced them to run with her to the parking lot, notwithstanding the fact of Delight van Buskirk's advanced age.

But people were watching. Even so, Mother Grey made her dignified retreat at such a high rate of speed that she bumped into Canon Arthur Spelving in the hallway.

"Dear Lord, Mother Grey, isn't this awful," he said.

"Awful," she said.

"How are you holding up, dear?" he said. "Is there anything I can do?"

"No thank you, Father. I'll be fine as soon as I can get my delegates home."

"I can't even begin to deal with the fact that the bishop is dead," he said. "I keep wondering what's going to happen to all our plans now, and where we go from here. It will probably be another year before we can pass the budget revision."

She hadn't even thought of it, but yes, she had all but promised to speak on Canon Spelving's amendment, and now with the death of the bishop the whole convention was up in the air. Whatever happened next would depend on the Standing Committee. "Arthur, I have to go," she said.

"Someone from the committee will get in touch with you," he called after her.

The lay delegates from St. Bede's were still where she had left them, crouched in half-darkness under the shadow of the balcony, three on the aisle. Phyllis Wagonner was not crying, Mother Grey was relieved to see. Delight van Buskirk was absorbed in her knitting. She seemed to have done four more inches on the sweater she was making for her great-grandson. If the death of the bishop disturbed or upset her, she gave no sign.

Ralph Voercker was calmly eating the last of St. Dinarius's cream puffs.

"How are you doing, Vinnie?" said Phyllis. "Was it awful?"

"Well, yes," said Mother Grey, "it was awful. Poor Bishop Wealle." Phyllis patted her hand and then began to tidy the things in her lap, shuffling convention papers and poking in the contents of her tote bag. Powdered sugar was all over everything. Mrs. van Buskirk folded her work.

Ralph licked his fingers and said cheerfully, "At least he can't make you close St. Bede's now."

"Try to behave as though you had good sense, Ralph," Mrs. van Buskirk muttered. "His Grace had nothing against St. Bede's."

"Ralph, what are you talking about?" said Mother Grey. Of course, he probably hadn't any idea. *I shouldn't get angry at him*, she thought, and then, for the hundredth time, *I shouldn't have let him come.* But she had needed three delegates, and there wasn't anyone else; the other two old ladies had gone to the nursing home last month.

And there was no requirement that the delegates have all their buttons.

If only there were some way for Mother Grey to turn Ralph into a human being. Well, of course, Ralph was a child of God like anyone else, but there was something missing. For one thing, he had never shown a sincere regard for anyone other than himself. Except, sometimes, Mother Grey. She sighed. There was always hope.

Ralph shifted his bulk in the protesting auditorium seat and wiped his hands on the knees of his pants. "In fact, I guess I'd have to say it's a good thing, Mother," he said.

"A good thing?" she said, trying to get aboard his train of thought. "What is?"

"Bishop Wealle being dead," he said. "Whoever the next bishop is, he'll probably understand what a great work you're doing in Fishersville and let you stay at St. Bede's."

Mother Grey was dumbstruck. She thrust her hands deep into her jacket pockets and drew in her breath to upbraid him, as soon as she could think of a penetrating rebuke, and it was then that the fingers of her left hand closed around a pair of gold-rimmed glasses.

Bishop Wealle's glasses. Something had happened to cause them to come off while he was drinking from the fountain where she found them. Something. The thing that had caused him to go crawling around in the cloakroom and catch the chain of his cross on the table leg . . .

Ralph was smiling up at her from his patched

auditorium seat of gold velvet and cheap monkscloth, his face benevolent. All at once she saw it: Ralph, her Ralph, cheerfully strangling Bishop Wealle for the greater glory of St. Bede's as he bent to drink from the fountain. Seizing the old churchman's lifeless body by the heels, dragging it into the cloakroom, singing softly to himself. A hymn tune, perhaps; *"Welcome Happy Morning, Age to Age Shall Say."* Thinking, "Mother will be so pleased."

For she suddenly remembered seeing a smudge of white powder across the dead bishop's chest.

Had she seen it? Or was she imagining it now? But the idea was absurd. Ralph could never hurt anyone. Even the suicide attempts had been fake, she was almost certain.

"Are you all right, Vinnie?" said Phyllis.

"I'm very tired," she said. *And I'm not up to two encounters in the same evening with Detective David Dogg.* Of course he would have to be told about the glasses, but not right this very minute.

"Can we go home now?" said Mrs. van Buskirk.

"Let's go home," said Mother Lavinia Grey, brushing her hands together.

5

Carefully, so as not to smudge any finger-prints, Mother Grey put the suspicious glasses in an envelope for Detective Dogg as soon as she got home to the rectory. A machine answered in his gravelly voice when she called the number on his card, "This is Detective David Dogg, I am away from my desk right now, please leave a message when you hear the beep." She told the machine about the glasses, couching her news in terms that would give the impression that she had found them when she got home, without actually lying about it.

Not that she really thought there would be any truths to be revealed by fingerprints. The bishop's death had been accidental. (Ralph, ripping off the bishop's glasses with a snarl of malice, crushing his neck, dragging him . . .)

In the morning the telephone rang as she was brushing her teeth, but it was Canon Spelving and not David Dogg. The funeral would be Wednesday, he said, to leave time for an autopsy, and after that it would be decided when and where to call the convention together again. Much business still needed to be voted upon. The question of the budget had to be decided, and now another bishop had to be elected. But the Standing Committee wanted to bury the bishop before resuming the business of the convention. "That can all be done with a president pro tempore," he said. "It will take time to find good candidates for the office of bishop."

For a moment Mother Grey had the idea that Canon Spelving was seizing the opportunity to make his move. But no, if that were the case, he would be calling and politicking at his fellow members on the powerful diocesan committees, not bending the ear of one little parish priest. Although it was still early. Maybe the committee members were next on his list of calls.

Mother Grey came out of these speculations to hear Canon Spelving repeating the day and hour of the bishop's funeral. It was to take place in the Trinity Cathedral in Trenton.

"How is his family taking it?" she asked him.

"There's no family left," said Father Spelving. "Didn't you know? He lost his wife and son years and years ago."

"How sad," she said.

"Yes," he said. "A tragedy all around. Well, then, I'll see you on Wednesday, Mother."

"Good-bye till then," she said, and hung up.

Since the convention was not to meet that morning, Mother Grey was free to take up her normal round of duties and pursuits. She showered, dressed in her scruffies, fed and watered Towser, and went to the church to check on things. But the face of the dead bishop stared out of all the dark corners. *I should paint the walls white*, she thought. *Ralph will help me.*

She sat down in the front pew. The old varnish was black and crazed; all the woodwork needed stripping and refinishing. That would bring some light in here. She was beginning to accept the fact that the bishop had been murdered. He must have been. How else could his glasses have gotten into the drinking fountain?

Had Ralph Voercker killed the bishop?

She stared at the brass Communion rail and thought of Ralph helping to polish it, of his large strong hands. She thought of the bishop's neck.

The bishop had been murdered, and almost certainly by someone at the convention. No random derelict had done it.

Because the only two ways to get to the downstairs lobby of the War Memorial Auditorium were the two sets of steps, and both sets passed directly in front of the tables that had been set up to process the registration of convention-goers. These tables had been constantly manned by a phalanx of vigilant Episcopalians from the time the doors were opened to the time the body was found. No wandering bum or junkie could have escaped that row of eyes.

It was almost as certain that the murder had

been done by someone whose life had been touched by the bishop's life, someone who bore him a grudge or hoped to get him out of the way. Unless, of course, it had been some sudden and groundless aberration of a deranged mind.

A mind not unlike Ralph's.

A noise of creaking echoed in the empty church as the front door opened. *I really must oil those hinges*, Mother Grey thought, and turned to see Detective David Dogg enter in a small whirlwind of dry leaves.

"Good morning, Detective Dogg," she called in the heartiest voice she could muster, sailing confidently down the aisle to meet him, putting out her hand.

"Morning, Reverend," he said, and they shook. His hand was warm and dry, a pleasant feeling, but his eyes were like blue lasers.

"I have the glasses for you in an envelope back at the rectory," she said, and then, somewhat lamely, "They were in my pocket." Oh, if only she had given him the wretched things the night before. No amount of inconvenience could have been worse than having him here on her own turf, drilling into her with those eyes.

"In your pocket, yes," he said. "That's one of the things I wanted to ask you about. Where were these glasses, exactly, when you found them originally? I didn't quite understand, from your telephone message."

"The glasses were in the fountain," she said.

"Behind the edge of it. You couldn't see them unless you were taking a drink."

"And so you took a drink from the fountain, and there they were."

"Yes. That's right."

Dogg took out a rough diagram of the lower lobby of the War Memorial Auditorium and pointed with a pencil to the northernmost of the two rectangles marked *drinking fountain*. "Would this be the fountain?" he said.

She said, "Yes. How did you know?"

"There was physical evidence," said Dogg, making a mark. "I'm not at liberty to discuss it."

"Oh," she said. "Well, if you'll come with me, I'll get the glasses for you. They're next door at the rectory."

"There's something else I need from you too," he said as she locked up the church. "I'd like you to let me have that coat you wore last night, if you would, please. The one with the powder on it."

"Good heavens."

"The boys from the lab want to run a few tests."

"Boys!?"

"Forensic pathology. They want me to get everybody's coat," he said. "Or sweater. Whatever."

"Aren't there any women in forensic pathology?"

"Look, I have a warrant," he said. "I have to take your coat. The hiring practices of the Trenton police department are not the point."

"It's just that I haven't got another one," she said. In a minute she would start whining at him.

Oh, what would she do? It had taken her weeks of prowling the secondhand stores to find that gray suit, and it had been available only because some size-six investment banker in Bucks County had decided to abandon the Wall Street life and send her gray flannel uniforms to a consignment shop in New Hope. Forty dollars for a Joseph Banks suit, and only slightly used. "When can I have it back?"

"I'll do the best I can," he said. "You need it Sunday?"

"No, we wear vestments," she said. "But when the convention reconvenes—well, I suppose I could wear a cardigan sweater." How humiliating.

Towser, locked in the kitchen to save the hardwood floors from his messes, began to bark as soon as she put the key in the door to the rectory. Dave Dogg squirmed uncomfortably. "He doesn't bite," she told the detective.

"You live here?" he said. It was true that there wasn't any furniture to speak of on the first floor. It takes time to get one's living quarters just right.

"Yes, I live here," she said. "By the way, I was wondering. Have you talked to the people from the Registration Committee? One or another of them was at the tables in front of the door the whole time. They would have seen whoever went up and down the stairs."

"We have their statements, Reverend. I take it you're not insisting it was an accident anymore."

She shrugged. "With his glasses in the fountain,

it just seems . . . It's hard to visualize, that's all. Would you like a cup of coffee? I made it about half an hour ago."

"Thanks," he said. "I would." She led him across the tarpaulin, through the paint cans, and into the kitchen, a sorry sight, but at least the dishes were clean and the garbage taken care of. The bishop's eyeglasses, if such they were, were on the counter beside the stove. Mother Grey gave them to Detective Dogg. Towser was jumping all over him.

"Down, Towser!" she said. "Bad dog. Shall I put him in the basement?"

"No, he's okay," said the detective. "I like dogs. What happened to his leg?"

She said, "Probably hit by a truck. We never knew. The dog appeared on the church steps one Sunday morning with its leg hurt, and when I took him to Dr. Dresner, she found that it was broken in several places. She put a pin in it. She said to keep him from running around. That's why he stays in the kitchen."

"He's not even your dog?"

"I ran an ad in the *Clarion*. I put posters all over town. I don't know whose dog he is, if he isn't mine."

The detective looked at the dog's little corner with its newspapers, checked out the floor, the ceiling, the cracked windows, the stained walls, taking in everything. Mother Grey thought of all the newspaper crime stories she had read where the investigating officers felt moved to comment on the housekeeping habits of one of the principals. *The house was a mess, Your Honor. We knew right away she was a murderer. And you should see what she does to strange dogs.* She said, "As you can see, the rectory needs a lot of work, but it's coming along. Have a chair."

"Thanks," he said, and plopped himself into one of her treasures, an oak chair she had found last month at the flea market. Towser put his nose in the detective's lap.

"How do you like your coffee?"

"Black," he said. "Thanks."

She poured out two mugs, put some milk in hers, unplugged the coffee maker, and sat down across from him.

"You live here by yourself?" he asked.

"Yes," she said. "I could probably use a housekeeper, but the parish can't support one."

"I mean, you're not married or anything. But I guess a priest wouldn't be married."

She smiled. "I'm not a nun, detective. Priests in the Episcopal Church have always been able to marry." She took a drink of coffee and wondered whether it wouldn't have been better to make a fresh pot. It seemed bitter. "I was married, but that was years ago, before I was called to the priesthood."

"What happened?"

"My husband died." She had learned finally to compress the experience—eight months in hospital waiting rooms, knitting her grief and terror into sweaters that she could never look at again,

Stephen's pain, her almost final crisis of faith—into those three words. "Seven years ago next month."

"You don't look old enough for that," he said.

"I am, though." What did he mean? How should she look? What did a widow look like? "I'm thirty-five."

"You could have fooled me," he said.

"Why would I want to fool you?"

There was an awkward silence. Detective Dogg blushed deeply. *This is getting us nowhere,* Mother Grey thought. *I might as well seize the bull by the horns.*

"So tell me about Bishop Wealle," she said. "What was the cause of death? Has the autopsy been completed? What did they find?"

He opened his portfolio and took out a notepad. He said, "I want to ask about the delegates who were at the convention with you last night. How well do you know them?"

Apparently she was supposed to tell him things, and not the other way around. "They are my parishioners," she said primly. *My little flock.* "I've scarcely been here eight months, and I didn't know any of them before I came here. But it seems unlikely to me that one of them would kill the bishop. How did he die? Exactly?"

Again he ignored the question. "I wonder if you could just fill me in on as much of these people's backgrounds as you can, where they come from, what they do for a living, what connection they might have with Bishop Wealle, that sort of thing."

Mother Grey sighed, and took a long drink of coffee, and went on to tell him almost everything she knew about Delight, Phyllis, and Ralph. None of them, as far as she knew, had even the remotest connection with Bishop Wealle.

"Delight van Buskirk lives up the hill in an old farmhouse her grandfather built. You can't miss it; it's right in the middle of Fisher's Pointe Condominiums. All that land used to belong to her and her husband before he died. I think they had a dairy farm. She's very old, at least ninety; she told me she was here before the umbrella factory.

"I'm almost sure Mrs. van Buskirk didn't know the bishop. I can't imagine that she would have had a grudge against him. And even if there were some reason why she might want to kill him, it just seems very unlikely to me that an old lady who has led a blameless life would ruin her hopes of salvation at the last minute by murdering the Bishop of New Jersey. Even if she were physically able to do it."

"Okay," said Dogg. "And the other two?"

"Phyllis Wagonner runs the library here in town. She might be strong enough to kill the bishop, I suppose, depending, of course, on how he died—?" When Dogg made no response, Mother Grey continued. "Phyllis is a good friend of mine, actually, aside from being a parishioner. We play together sometimes."

"What do you play?" said Detective Dogg.

"Chamber music. Baroque string trios, mostly." Mother Grey had recommended to Phyllis that she work on her violin skills and join the chamber music group she had formed with Dr. Dresner, partly for therapy and partly for herself, because it was more fun with three. As it turned out, Phyllis's house was a wonderful place to play chamber music, an old Victorian mansion built by her father's family. Phyllis was all by herself there now, but the music room had a lovely sound quality, and there was a very fine piano, though it was way out of tune. "Phyllis plays violin," she told the detective. "It's hard sometimes finding someone to play with at your own level of expertise." Come to think of it, it was Mother Grey's turn tonight to host one of their sessions. Was there anything in the house for dinner?

"I know what you mean," said the detective. "I play softball myself."

Maybe Phyllis Wagonner had murdered the bishop because he was prochoice. What an idea. To take her mind off this foolishness, Mother Grey tried to imagine the detective in a softball uniform, little beer belly and all, standing out in center field with his hands on his knees. Chewing tobacco.

"If you want to talk to Phyllis," she said, "you'll find her at the library. It's open Saturday mornings. It's on High Street."

"And this other person," Dogg prompted.

Now they were on slippery ground. Mother Grey paused to think for a moment. She wondered how to present Ralph as other than an obvious psychopath. "Ralph Voercker," she said at last. "My acolyte."

"An altar boy," Dogg translated.

"Yes."

"What sort of person is he?"

"He's a tremendous help to me, detective. I don't know how I could carry on the work of St. Bede's without him."

Dogg made a little note. "And what does he do for a living? I'm assuming that 'altar boy' isn't a paid position."

She said, "Ralph is between jobs right now. But we're certain to find something for him quite soon. More coffee?"

"Thanks, no," said the detective. He stood up. "Where is Mr. Voercker living?"

"At the group home for disturbed . . . He's living with some other young men over on Main Street, number fourteen. It's a big blue house. He has absolutely no connection with the bishop. I'm sure none of them has any connection at all with the bishop."

"Can you think of anyone who might profit by Bishop Wealle's death?"

An image flashed in her mind of Arthur Spelving arrayed in a bishop's miter and cope. "No," she said quickly.

"How about you, then?"

"What?"

"Did you have any connection with the bishop?"

"No. None. I mean, he was my bishop." He was making her nervous again. There seemed to be two David Doggs, she thought, one the icy professional investigator and the other the nice guy who loved animals and enjoyed your coffee. But which was real? Did he assume the professional air in the line of duty, or did he pretend to be nice to throw his suspects off guard?

"One other thing I wanted to ask you," he said. He stood up, and out of his portfolio he drew a small plastic bag containing a black and gold lipstick case. "Is this the lipstick you lost?"

"Looks like it," she said. "Rose of Picardy. Can I have it back?"

"We'd like to keep it for now, but I did want you to identify it if you could. And also this." He took out another flat plastic bag, this one holding a piece of letter-size paper, ecru with brown printing, folded in three; it appeared to be a rumpled copy of the latest Fishersville Chamber of Commerce tourism promotion flyer, the one with the picture of St. Bede's.

"That's one of the flyers we took with us to the convention to help drum up support for St. Bede's. The church is a local institution, really. They may put it on the National Register of Historic Places next year. Then we can get a low-cost loan to fix the roof, if we're still . . . Where did you find it?"

"But it's your flyer. Right?"

"Everyone in the delegation from St. Bede's had a packet of them to give out. Mrs. van Buskirk even gave a handful to Father Spelving. I didn't give the bishop a flyer, if that's what you need to know. As I told you before, I never got a chance to talk to him at all. You don't mean to tell me it's a clue."

"How many of these flyers did each of the delegates have to give away?"

"I'm afraid we didn't count them. Everyone just took a big handful."

"Right. Thanks for the coffee, then, Reverend. I'm gonna get going. I want you to be sure to call me if you think of anything else."

"Let me see you out." On his way to the door, he seemed to be looking disapprovingly at her renovations.

"You know, Reverend, you really shouldn't leave all this paint thinner sitting around by the bottom of the stairs," he said.

"Oh, I know, but there's just so much to do." Had they found the Chamber of Commerce handout on the bishop's body? If so, how had it gotten there? Why wouldn't this man answer any of her questions? Why was he talking about paint thinner?

"It's dangerous, is why I mention it. One of those rags could go up. Ever hear of spontaneous combustion?"

"I'll be sure and take care of it," she said, and she really did mean to. But first she had to close the dog into the kitchen, and then she had to drive out to the nursing home for a pastoral visit, and then she had to shop for supper for herself and the other members of the string trio, and after that she had to run over her part in the new piece they were going to try to play tonight. And so time went on, and the paint mess remained, and so, in the back of her mind, did the questions.

6

The paint rags were still untouched when Phyllis Wagonner appeared at the rectory door, fiddle case in hand, to engage in an evening of dining and music-making, followed closely by Dr. Sheila Dresner.

Usually they met at Phyllis's house. Phyllis had a piano and could play it, and so there were pieces they could do at Phyllis's that they couldn't at the rectory. Also, things were nicer there; Phyllis had money; she served expensive snacks; she even seemed to enjoy cooking sometimes. Occasionally they would arrive and find that Phyllis had whipped up something out of Julia Child. Creature comforts. Mother Grey lived an ascetic life ordinarily, by choice she hoped, but perhaps it was through laziness.

In that sense, it was better to have the sessions at the rectory. For when they went to Phyllis's house, Mother Grey was reminded of the pleasures of the flesh. Fine china. Soft chairs. Good acoustics. Bowls of potpourri here and there in discreet places, rather than the undiscovered little gifts from Towser that perfumed the air of the rectory.

Once you entered her iron gate, the very approach to Phyllis's house reeked of generations of money; in the summer it was the roses and the grass that she paid a boy to cut; in the fall, the smell of the old boxwood hedge, a bitter smell, almost unpleasant, almost animal.

When Phyllis invited her into the cool hall with the flowered wallpaper, Mother Grey would see herself, and sometimes Phyllis, in the mirrored hat stand, overflowing with umbrellas. They were Wagonner's Umbrellas. She would feel the softness of the old carpets, admire the window treatments and the furniture.

She would look the piano over to see whether Phyllis had been taking proper care of it. "Oh, no, Vinnie, I forgot to have it tuned again, but Modine did a nice job of polishing it, don't you think?" It smelled of lemon oil but sounded flat. Mother Grey saw her face reflected in it. This house had an enormous number of mirrors; the Wagonners must have been very pretty people.

The many exquisite objects arranged about Phyllis's house covered every flat surface: oriental-looking porcelain bowls filled with things like seashells, arrangements of glass paperweights, needlepoint pillows depicting improbably well behaved dogs. If Mother Grey commented on any of these—"What lovely paperweights!"—Phyllis said simply, "They were Mother's." In contrast, Mother Grey had only one thing that had belonged to her own mother: her cello. Grandmother Dales had given the cello to her daughter as a wedding present. A curious wedding present! The intention, as Mother Grey understood it, had been to encourage the new bride to retain her position as cellist with the Washington Symphony.

Indeed the cello was the only thing of real monetary value that Mother Grey had. Her furniture, the little bit there was of it, was comfortable in its way, but if she were to lose it today, she could replace it tomorrow at any one of the nearby flea markets. She owned two pairs of shoes, three counting her hiking boots. Her clothes were the bare minimum required to give warmth and decorously cover her nakedness. It was important to her to strip away all attachment to worldly things. For this reason she felt that spending time at Phyllis's house, where all the objects sang to her, was corrupting.

So occasionally she insisted that the trio meet at the rectory. They almost never played at Sheila's, and that was chiefly because everyone hated the smell of Sheila's husband's cigars. He was an excellent man; Sheila loved him deeply; his one vice, or the only one Sheila ever mentioned, was the cigars, rank stinky things that he insisted on smoking in the evenings whether or not anyone within range minded.

Sheila was the doctor who took care of Mother Grey's dog. She was Mother Grey's friend too, and

Mother Grey often wished that she could have joined the church as well, since they needed bodies so badly, but Sheila was Jewish. There were two schools of thought amongst the Episcopal clergy on the subject of evangelizing Jews. Mother Grey was of the school that regarded it as impolite, presumptuous, perhaps even pushy.

"Come in," said Mother Grey. "Let me have your coats." The women put down their instrument cases while she hung the coats in the closet under the stairs.

"Really, Vinnie," said Phyllis, "you ought to hire a painter to finish this work. You're never going to get time to do it yourself."

"Maybe Ralph can do it," Mother Grey said. "He works for nothing." She reproached herself for exploiting him, but Ralph didn't seem to mind; working at the church was another excuse not to go out looking for a job.

Dinner was on the kitchen table, canned chili with a little extra cumin, for a gourmet touch, and corn bread from a mix. Almost as an afterthought, Mother Grey had put together a tossed salad. Mother Grey hated salad, but other people seemed to require it. Until the renovations were complete in the dining and living rooms, Mother Grey chose to conduct her entertainments and larger counseling sessions in the rectory kitchen, since it was a big room where people felt at ease around the table.

Sheila made a fuss over Towser, who seemed to

be glad to see her. They hadn't seen each other since the day she took off his cast.

With a sigh of something between relief and anticipation, Mother Grey sat down to her plate of chili. She was looking forward to a pleasant evening with friends, where no church business would be discussed or thought of. But alas, it was not to be. Sheila Dresner had read about the bishop's death in the morning paper.

"What will you people do for a bishop now?" she said.

"I don't know," said Mother Grey. "The old bishop isn't even cold, and now the police are after us. Phyllis, did that man from Trenton come to see you this morning? He was collecting articles of clothing."

"Detective Dogg," said Phyllis, with a little smile. "Yes, he did. I gave him a blouse and skirt."

"What did you think of him?" asked Mother Grey.

"For a short, freckled, balding, red-headed policeman, I thought he was very attractive," said Phyllis.

Attractive? It was an idea that hadn't occurred to her before, at least not on a conscious level.

"Clothing?" Sheila Dresner was enormously interested. "He wanted your clothing? Who is this person?" she said. "Is he single? Is he a transvestite? Or what?" Single men were of interest to Sheila because, being herself happily married, she believed that her friends would be better off with men of their own. At least, that was what she always said. Maybe the truth was that she was insecure about Jake, cigars and all, and feared in her secret heart that unattached women, even her friends, might put the moves on him.

"He's investigating the bishop's death," Mother Grey said. "He might be attractive. Depends on what sort of person you like."

"He was very interested in Vinnie's friend Ralph," said Phyllis. "Vinnie, do you have any cheese? I like grated cheese on my chili."

"Only Parmesan," said Mother Grey. "It isn't good on chili."

"Ralph!" said Sheila. "You mean that great big geek who keeps trying to kill himself? Is he a suspect?"

"He's not a geek," Mother Grey insisted. "He just seems to crave an unusual amount of attention."

Phyllis said, "You must have laid it on a bit thick with the altar boy routine. I take it that you were trying to paint Ralph as a harmless . . ."

"Nonentity. A harmless nonentity. Trying not to draw any attention to him whatever."

"I don't think you quite succeeded, Vinnie," said Phyllis.

"So how about it," said Sheila. "Is he single or what?"

"Ralph?" said Mother Grey.

"The policeman. Is his name really Dog?"

"Dogg. With two g's. I don't know if he's single. What did you tell him about Ralph, Phyllis?"

"I had to tell him about the suicide attempt. He

would have found out anyway from the Fishersville police. I painted him as a very nonviolent person."

"Well, he is."

"Right. I know."

There was a long silence while the women ate their chili, each absorbed in her own thoughts. Towser got up and turned around a couple of times, rattling his toes on the linoleum, and then settled down again with his chin on Mother Grey's foot.

"What did you tell him about me?" Phyllis asked finally.

"Who you were, and where to find you, was about all. Surely you don't think you're a suspect. That's just his way, you know. He makes everyone feel like that."

"Of course I'm not a suspect," said Phyllis. "He's just here in Fishersville trying to make time with you, Vinnie."

Sheila burst into gales of laughter. "I want to meet this man," she said.

"No, you don't," said Mother Grey. "You don't actually want to meet this man." *He has hard eyes.* "Detective Dogg is just an ordinary police officer doing his job. Right now his job seems to be finding somebody to blame for the death of the bishop. No doubt he would be equally happy with Ralph or either one of us. He's probably under a lot of pressure, you know; the bishop was an important man."

"Why doesn't he go after the other three hundred or however many other people who were there at the convention?" said Sheila.

"I don't know," said Mother Grey. "Why us? I guess you have to start an investigation somewhere. But maybe there's some other reason. Did Ralph mess up your blouse?"

"What!?" said Sheila.

"With powdered sugar," said Mother Grey. "Ralph stole Father Bingley's cream puffs and then proceeded to smear them all over everyone in sight."

"And Dave Dogg thought it was cocaine," said Phyllis, beginning to laugh.

"Father Bingley!" cried Sheila. "Isn't he the one who offered to send the van for your parishioners? So he's involved in this. What a riot! Why don't you pin the murder on him?"

The idea of Bingley in the slammer was irresistible. They all howled with laughter, until Mother Grey realized that she was having hysterics and put her head in her hands, trying to take slow, deep breaths.

The general hilarity subsided. "I'm sorry," said Sheila. "You must feel terrible. You were the one who found the body, weren't you? That must have been awful."

"True, Sheila, it wasn't very nice," said Mother Grey. "I stepped on his hand, as a matter of fact." Her chili seemed to have grown cold. Cold beans. "Can we talk about something else? At least until I've finished eating."

"You poor thing," said Sheila. "Yes, of course. Oh, I have some news about your dog."

"Towser?" said Mother Grey. The tail thumped on the floor.

"There was a picture of him in one of my professional journals this month. At least, there was a picture of one of his breed."

"Breed?" said Mother. "My dog has a breed? Anyway, Sheila, you know he's not my dog."

"It's a new breed. Petit Basset Griffon de Vendimes. They call them peebie-jeevies. The AKC didn't begin to recognize them as a breed until last year."

"What makes you think Towser is a heebie-jeebie?" said Phyllis, wiping her eyes with her paper napkin.

"Look at this," said Sheila, taking a folded page from a magazine out of her purse. The picture on it looked very like Towser on a good day. "I saw this picture, and I said, 'There's Vinnie's Towser.' They were developed in Europe by crossing a basset with some other thing, I think it was an otter hound."

"My guess would be that Towser was the result of a volunteer effort by a couple of local dogs who happened to be of those breeds," said Phyllis.

"It's possible. The thing is," said Sheila, "these animals are enormously valuable."

"Are you telling me that Towser is worth a lot of money?"

"Not without papers, of course. But he might be worth money to someone."

"His rightful owner," said Mother Grey.

"Could be. Anyway, if I hear of one missing, I'll let you know right away."

They withdrew to the library, formerly the upstairs front bedroom, where there were three straight chairs. There they tuned up and for several hours played string trios, without discussing the death of the bishop or the attractions of Dave Dogg. Only once or twice did Mother Grey's mind return to the investigation, powdered sugar on the bishop's purple cassock, the noose tightening around Ralph, perhaps even around herself.

The string trio was improving. Or Mother Grey was getting less critical. It was beginning to sound a little more like music to her and less like hard work sweatily performed.

"I think we can take this show on the road pretty soon," said Sheila Dresner with a satisfied smile, as she packed away her violin. "But as for me, I have surgery tomorrow."

"And I have a christening, come to think of it," said Mother Grey, putting aside her cello. She tossed the remark off casually, as though babies were baptized at St. Bede's every week; the fact was that this baby was the first to cross the threshold of the old church in many years. His baptism was an enormously significant undertaking, requiring a good night's sleep beforehand.

But how could she sleep? The matter of the bishop's death so preoccupied her that Mother Grey found it difficult to do anything normal. The problem was that she felt helpless in the face of whatever it was that was going on. It was all very well to prayerfully consign events to God's hands. But passive obedience to divine will was more what nuns were all about. That was why she wasn't a nun. The Lord expects a little more moxie from priests. A priest takes charge. *Something must be done.*

As she was seeing Sheila to the door, a plan of action began to form in Mother Grey's mind. Her plan required the help of a librarian. "Let's have one more glass of sherry before you go," she said to Phyllis. "I want to talk to you about something."

"What's up?"

They retired to the kitchen and settled themselves with the bottle of Harvey's Bristol Cream. "You know that this Dogg person is zeroing in on Ralph," said Mother Grey.

"You think so?"

"And you know he couldn't possibly have done it." Mother Grey pronounced these words with ringing conviction, even though doubt gnawed deep in her vitals like a small animal.

"No, no," Phyllis agreed. "He couldn't possibly."

"What I propose," said Mother Grey, "is to do some investigating on my own."

"You, Vinnie?"

"Who else? Detective Dogg is going to think that Ralph is just another murderous geek and not look any further. Someone needs to go after the truth. I have some time to spare, if I let the rectory slide for a while longer. My plan is to begin by doing some research on the bishop."

"Whatever for?" said Phyllis.

"My theory is that whoever killed him is someone out of his past," said Mother Grey. "I want to find out everything I can about his past life. You can help me with your library connections. What's the best way to go about finding old newspaper stories on him, for instance?"

"Well," said Phyllis, "if you mean his life in the recent past, I can get whatever there is online. If you're talking long past, the best I can probably do is call the newspapers and get a list of dates when they might have run stories about him. That will mean loading up the microfilm reader and scanning every paper to find the story. Our microfilm reader won't print copies. If you want copies, you'll need to go to Trenton."

"Does the Trenton Public Library have a microfilm printer?"

"I think so. I know the state library has several of them. Tell you what. I'll get the list of dates for you, and you can go to Trenton and hunt out the stories."

"Okay. Good." Mother Grey smiled. "At least it will feel as if I'm doing something positive."

"Let me just ask you one question, Vinnie. Are you sure you want to dig around in the bishop's past? Maybe you might stir something up that would be better left alone."

"Phyllis, the man wasn't a mobster, for heaven's sake. He was a bishop."

"And yet someone killed him."

"Are you trying to tell me you think I'll be in some kind of danger?"

"I don't know what you'll be in. I just want you to think, that's all. Stop and reflect. This might not be something you really want to do. You might not like the results."

As she stared at her friend, trying to grasp what she was driving at, Mother Grey heard a knock at the front door. She went to answer it, stepping with practiced feet around the cans, trays, and paint rollers.

On the doorstep stood a woman Mother Grey thought she had seen before, perhaps one of the tenants from Horace Burkhardt's apartment building across the street. She had two children with her, the baby in her arms and the little boy gripping one of her plump legs and staring at Mother Grey. As cold as it was outside, the woman was dressed in shorts and a thin blouse that strained at the buttons. An amazing tattoo adorned her left thigh, some winged creature in four colors. Her long blond hair, which hung in strings around her face, was held tight in the grip of the baby. "Can I use your phone?" the woman said. "He's trying to kill me again."

7

"Who? Who's trying to kill you?" Mother Gray said. No one was out there that Mother Grey could see by the light of the streetlight. Dry leaves made a sound blowing over the sidewalk, and from the bar two blocks away came a peal of laughter, but the street seemed empty. Mother Grey pulled the woman and her children inside and closed the front door. Suddenly its thick beveled glass seemed inadequate.

"Rex," said the woman. The baby began to cry.

What time was it? Who was this person? Somewhat fuddled by sherry, Mother Grey had to force herself to think what to do next. The loud sound of the baby crying confused and distressed her. To think that she had a christening tomorrow and would be forced to hold one of these creatures in her arms!

Phyllis came charging through the kitchen door at the sound of the crying baby. As she opened the

door, Towser forced his way around her legs with
barks of great happiness and threw himself on the
little boy.

"Prince! Mom, it's Princie!" the boy cried.

"No, it ain't," the woman said.

Dog and boy began to roll on the floor. Mother
Grey, gazing at them amongst the paint cans,
thought, *I have to take charge of this somehow.*

"How old is your baby?" said Phyllis.

"Get away from that dog, it ain't Prince," the
woman said. "Three months. Please, I need to use
your phone. Rex is terrible drunk, and I have to
call the cops on him."

"The phone is over there," said Mother Grey.

The awful noise the baby was making didn't
seem to bother Phyllis. She walked right up to the
mother and said, "May I hold her?" just as if she
were asking for a favor.

The woman said, "Sure," and handed the baby
to her, first detaching its tiny fingers from her hair.
As the woman went to make her phone call, Phyllis, charmed, gazed into the baby's little noisy face
and uttered nonsense syllables in a high voice.

On the phone the woman was saying, "It's Saraleigh Kane, Jack. Could you come over? Rex is
crazy drunk again. He says he's gonna kill me."
Phyllis put the baby over her shoulder and gently
rocked it up and down, up and down. "I'm over
across the street," said Saraleigh Kane. "We
sneaked out the back while he was loading his
gun."

So Rex is out there with a loaded gun, thought

Mother Grey. She gazed out through the curtainless window into the dark but again could see no one. Phyllis crooned softly to the baby. It stopped crying.

"You have a way with babies," said Mother Grey.

"This is a lovely baby," said Phyllis.

"Hey, Princie." The boy chuckled, embracing the dog and thumping on him. "Mom, I know it's Prince. Here's the chewed place on his ear."

"It's not Prince. Prince got run over by a truck and killed. I told you."

"Are the police on their way?" said Mother Grey.

"They're coming. We'll just stay here till they take him away," said Saraleigh Kane. "If that's okay with you. Mind if I smoke?"

"No, no, feel free," said Mother Grey. "Come into the kitchen." *Where we can't be seen from the street.* "It's more comfortable in there. Does your husband get this way often? Has he considered AA? You know, there's a group that meets here at the church every Saturday night. If you like, I could see about getting him some counseling."

"Rex ain't my husband."

"I see," said Mother Grey.

"We was going to get married, but I dunno if I want to be married to him. He gets too crazy."

"You live across the street, don't you?"

"In the brown house. We're on the third floor." The woman took a deep drag on the cigarette and blew the smoke out of her nose. "He was sort of okay before, when he had a job, but with the umbrella factory closed, I just dunno."

Mother Grey felt a sudden stab of pity for this wretched woman, who was surely ten years younger than she was and yet carried herself as though she were ten years older. Two children, an abusive man, and a life of unimaginable misery. Mother Grey offered her hand. "I'm Mother Lavinia Grey," she said. "I'm the vicar of St. Bede's next door. This is Phyllis Wagonner; you may remember her from the library."

"Saraleigh Kane," said the woman, after an awkward pause, during which she seemed to be trying to remember how to interact socially with the sort of people who introduced themselves and shook hands. Saraleigh did not appear to recognize Phyllis, and Mother Grey suspected that she hadn't been in the library any more often than in the church.

There was a loud hammering on the front door. Saraleigh and her boy stiffened. Towser barked and snarled, and the baby cheesed on Phyllis's shoulder and started to scream again.

"I'll take them to my place until the coast is clear," Phyllis whispered. "We'll go out the back way."

"Can I take Prince, Mom?" the boy said.

"I told you, it ain't Prince," she said, and cuffed him on the ear. The whole howling mob began its exit as Mother Grey slipped through the kitchen door and into the front of the house.

Outside the front door a man stood framed in

the beveled glass. He was not large, not even particularly well-nourished, but he was mean looking.
His hair and beard were greasy and unkempt, and
the dirt under his fingernails could be seen from
ten feet away, through the glass and in the dim
light and everything. *No excuse for dirty nails*,
thought Mother Grey. *Why, the man doesn't even
have a job*. The sleeves were ripped off of his shirt,
perhaps for style, and his right biceps, hard and
stringy, bore a blue tattoo of initials in work as
crude as carving on a tree. He must have done it
himself. Why would anyone tattoo himself?

She fiddled with the doorknob until she felt a
slight movement of air that told her the back door
had opened and closed. Secure in the certainty
that the others had made good their escape, she
opened the front door wide.

The man's breath, sour with alcohol, almost
knocked her down. "My old lady here?" he said,
stepping in.

"I'm sorry," said Mother Grey. "What did you
say your name was?" The dog was perfectly silent.
Mother Grey wondered whether they had taken
him away after all.

"Rex Perskie," he said, and shambled into the
paint cans. "I know my old lady is here, I seen her
come in." The shirt he wore was loose enough to
hide a gun if he had tucked one into his waistband.
Mother Grey wondered whether he had. "Where is
she?" he said. "I'm gonna kill her ass. She didn't
give me no goddamned supper."

Perhaps it was a bad time to suggest the AA

meeting. Yes, the butt of a revolver was peeping coyly out of the back of his pants. "I can see that you must be very hungry," said Mother Grey. "Can I offer you some chili?"

"Huh?"

"Come on out to the kitchen, and I'll fix you something to eat. I'll put it in the microwave."

He pondered her offer for a moment, and then said, "Thanks," and went reeling into the kitchen. She gave him a plate of hot food. While he was busy eating, she surreptitiously put the half-empty sherry bottle away in the cupboard out of sight, just in case he took a notion to get any drunker. It was then that she noticed that the dog was cringing silently under the stove.

There was yet another knock at the door.

It was Officer Kreevitch, looking for Rex.

"In the kitchen, Jack," Mother Grey said to him, "eating supper. You know, he's carrying a gun in the back of his pants."

Kreevitch snickered. "Gonna blow his hind end off one of these days. Good old Rex."

"Friend of yours, is he?" said Mother Grey.

"He's okay," said Officer Kreevitch. "He never hurts anybody. I'll take him down to the lockup, and he'll be fine in the morning."

"I distinctly heard him threaten to kill his wife," she said.

"Don't worry about it. He don't mean it. He used to be a cop; we kind of look out for him." He pushed open the kitchen door. "Yo, Rex. Time to take a little rest."

But Rex was not at the kitchen table where Mother Grey had left him. Rather he was out on the back doorstep, vomiting on the chrysanthemums. Kreevitch followed him out to where he stood leaning over the porch railing. In a single gesture, impressive in its smoothness, the police officer put one arm around Perskie's heaving shoulder and with the other hand removed the gun. Sure enough, it looked like a service revolver.

"Come on, buddy," said Kreevitch. "Time to go." The two of them then went out of sight around the house, Kreevitch murmuring encouragement, Perskie stopping from time to time to retch.

When she could no longer hear them, Mother Grey felt a push against her legs. It was Towser/Prince. She put her hand on his collar, thinking he might run away, but what he seemed to want to do was bark and bark and bark at the retreating back of the man who surely was his former master.

Rain fell during the night, and when Mother Grey put Towser on the lead and took him for their predawn exercise, it was wet out and very cold. She would have liked to run, but Towser was still limping from his injuries. If he didn't appear to enjoy it so much, she wouldn't have taken him out at all.

They went along the riverbank in the pearly half-light, past the umbrella factory and down toward the wing dam. As they walked along the tracks, the ducks and geese crouching in the weeds by the river complained at them in their loud voices. The ducks of Fishersville never seemed to fly south. Maybe this was the South, as far as they were concerned. All at once two white ducks rose up and flew over their heads, and Mother Grey thought of Saint Hilda of Whitby.

Towser stopped to urinate on an old Long Island Rail Road snowplow parked on a rusty sidetrack. These were not, of course, LIRR tracks but a hobby line, run by a couple of rail fans who collected cars the way one would collect electric trains. The plow was a curiosity. Probably the rail fans had never used it; New Jersey didn't get a lot of snow. Bad words were written on the outside. Inside, a small group of the homeless seemed to be asleep. The plow afforded some shelter. Mother Grey sighed. Winter was certainly coming.

Towser snuffled at an old coat crumpled in the mud. Mother Grey pulled him away from it and moved on down the track. Her first thought was that it was rude to wake sleeping people, but her next was that here was a ministry, a duty to be performed, although she wasn't certain what it might involve. Homeless people by the riverbank! She should do something about getting them shelter, sobering them up if that was what was required. Not right now, of course, but after church she could casually stroll by and find out who they were and what they needed.

As the sun came up over the dark hills to the east of town, Mother Grey began to think of turning back. Then she heard in the distance a sound like that of a chain saw, and suddenly there was a great agitation of ducks and wildlife. A scarfed and helmeted young man on a dirt bike roared down upon them.

Mother Grey and her dog moved out of the way just in time to avoid a collision. The youth sped away, but it was definitely time to go. Musing on the disagreeable inclination of the young to make loud noises, Mother Grey turned off the track that followed the river and made for Delio's.

"Aren't you supposed to fast before Mass, Mother Vinnie?" Horace Burkhardt, having his own doughnut and reading the Sunday *Trentonian*, caught her buying breakfast.

"We don't fast," she said. "But I can't stop to eat with you, either, Horace, because I left Towser tied up on the doorstep."

"You two go for a walk?"

"Down by the river. It was lovely. The leaves are nearly all gone."

"I know how they feel," the old man said. "I hate to see another winter coming."

"You'll see lots more winters," said Mother Grey, but maybe it wasn't true. "At least you and I have roofs over our heads."

"Tough to get anybody to fix 'em." Horace was a landlord; he owned a number of properties around town. The crumbling apartment house where he lived, across the street from the rectory, was one of them.

"That reminds me, Horace, do you know anybody who will work on a slate roof? Cheaply, if possible, but I need someone good."

"Pete Willard used to do my roofs. He was good with slate, but he passed last January. All my old classmates. One by one, we wither up and drop off."

Evidently Horace was in a mood. She patted him on the shoulder and took her breakfast and her newspaper home to the rectory kitchen.

LOST: Petit Basset Griffon de Vendimes. Male, cream tipped with gray. Answers to "Hercules." $100 reward.

Might be Towser, thought Mother Gray. *He answers to most anything.* "Don't you, Towser?" she said to him, asleep with his head on her foot again. Thump, thump went the tail. These mornings were becoming companionable, now that the dog was healing up and not quite so much trouble. She would miss him when the real owners turned up.

She circled the ad, meaning to call the number as soon as services were over. It was time to prepare. This morning Henry Wellworth was to be baptized at the ten-thirty Eucharist.

Although she had almost forgotten about it in the hullabaloo surrounding the bishop's death, the christening was of great importance, almost greater for St. Bede's and Mother Grey than for the baby's family. Not only was this St. Bede's first baptism in thirty years, and Mother Grey's first ever, but this was the first new family to join the church since Mother Grey had come there.

That is, she hoped the Wellworths were actually going to join the church. They were young black professionals, just the sort of folks Mother Grey would like to see in her dream congregation. The husband, a West Indian, had been raised in the Church of England. "Of course, you'll need to become members of our family here at St. Bede's before I can baptize little Henry," Mother Grey had said to them, conjuring up an image of vast throngs of the blessed who met there every Sunday. At least Mr. and Mrs. Wellworth hadn't refused outright. Maybe someday St. Bede's would have a Sunday school again. Why, in only six years young Henry Wellworth would be ready for his first Communion.

While she showered and dressed, Mother Grey allowed herself to drift into dreams of ultimate success. White ducks flew over St. Bede's in her imagination, as Bishop Wealle's successor (Arthur Spelving, perhaps) came to administer the sacrament of Confirmation to all the lost sheep of the town, plus a few generous rich people to keep the thing going. Hundreds of the faithful packed the church, fifties of children thronged the Sunday school. They would build a parish hall for the AA and the senior citizens. They would start a day care center. The christening of Henry Wellworth was only the beginning. Mother Grey went over to the church to make her final preparations.

Mother Grey and Ralph had agreed to lay on the complete production for this one, with incense and the fanciest vestments. The church looked wonderful. Sunlight streamed through the stained-glass windows, and the dappled colors concealed many flaws. One could hardly tell how badly in want the old church was of varnish, paint, and plaster.

With a silent prayer of thanks for the good weather, Mother Grey gathered up the rain buckets and put them in the sacristy. Ralph, she no-

ticed, was getting really good at serving as an acolyte and no longer tripped over the skirts of his alb.

He came in from lighting the candles with his
eyes rolling. "Mother," he whispered. "I never
seen so many goddamned people."

Indeed, the baby's entire extended family
seemed to have come to the christening. The grave
and extremely proper old couple (she in the hat
and gloves, he in the white linen suit) would be the
husband's parents from Nassau. The citified
crowd must be the wife's people. Mrs. Wellworth
had mentioned relatives in New York. Everyone
was smiling. Henry was the first grandchild on
both sides.

The regulars were there too, of course, both of
them, and two pews in the very back were full of
strangers. Mother Grey suspected suddenly that
their presence had something to do with the death
of poor Bishop Wealle. She hoped that Phyllis
would make a special point of seeing that they put
something in the plate. Who were they? The police? The press? Up to that moment it had never
crossed her mind that the priest who had stepped
on the bishop's hand might be front-page tabloid
news.

But putting these thoughts behind her, Mother
Grey went on to pronounce the opening sentences.
All went well until the moment came for her to
urge little Henry, resting moistly in her arms, to
renounce Satan and all the spiritual forces of
wickedness. They were gathered around the bap-

tismal font by the door of the church, parents, god-parents, relatives, Phyllis, Mrs. van Buskirk, Ralph, and the whatever-they-weres from the back pews.

The door burst open.

There stood Rex Perskie, drunk again, or still drunk, wearing a T-shirt that said, "Eat Shit and Die."

"You," he snarled at Mother Grey.

She was so startled that she nearly dropped the baby.

"I must beg you to excuse me, Mr. Perskie," she said to him, pulling herself together. "We're conducting the Lord's business here. If you want to speak to me, you'll have to wait."

But he was not to be put off. As the assembled ones gaped in stupefaction—*They'll never come back here*, thought Mother Grey, *Oh no, oh no, this can't be happening*—Perskie screamed out a speech, peppered with obscenities, to the effect that Mother Grey had interfered unwarrantably in his personal affairs by suggesting to his significant other that he would benefit from alcoholism counseling:

"What is this shit! What the fuck is this shit!! Told my old lady I was a drunk, did you!! You fucking bitch!! You can fucking well mind your own goddamned fucking business!!"

Ralph Voercker moved in and grasped Perskie by his right arm, bringing it neatly and persuasively behind the man's back. "Mother Grey says she can't talk to you right now," said Ralph, and he took him outside and closed the door. But the damage was done. She knew she would never see the Wellworths again. This was the sort of thing they had left the city to get away from.

Then as the strangers pulled notebooks from their pockets and began furiously scribbling, her very worst fears were confirmed. Journalists. "The guy in the dress is pretty good with his hands," one of them muttered.

Somehow she got through the rest of the service. During her sermon, even shorter than the one she had planned, Ralph reappeared with mud on his alb. The strangers from the back pews did not take Communion. At last Mother Grey shook everyone's hand at the door, and they all went away, except for the journalists, who began to ask her things like how it felt to step on a dead bishop. When they saw Ralph come charging out of the sacristy, they, too, left.

"Ralph, my dear friend," she said, "I don't know what I would have done without you."

"Aw, Mother," he said, blushing. "Have a good day, okay?"

"You too," she said. As he went off down the street, she reflected that she really didn't know what she would have done without him. Or would do. What if Rex Perskie came back? What if the journalists came back? (No fear about the Wellworths; they would never come back.) If David Dogg were to charge her with murder, she might come in one Sunday to find the whole church packed with journalists. With a sigh she locked the door and then thought, *What if Ralph really murdered the bishop?*

9

The thought of her faithful acolyte wringing the bishop's neck—indeed, the horror of the bishop's murder in its entirety—was so thoroughly depressing to Mother Grey that to take her mind off it, she went straight home and called the number for the lost dog.

A woman answered, saying, "Hello," in a throaty voice. She sounded as if she had—money? class? a college education? speech training? Was it okay for a Christian person to think about social class? Anyway, Mother Grey had noticed that people in this part of the country who were below a certain socioeconomic level tended to pick up the phone and say, "H'lau." So she concluded, in much less time that it takes to tell it, that the woman who had lost her dog either had gone away to school, or didn't come from around here, or had money. (But not enough money to have the maid answer the phone.) Simultaneously she felt pangs of guilt for thinking about it at all.

There were no really rich people in Fishersville; it wasn't that sort of place. There were people like Phyllis who seemed to be comfortably off, but as far as Mother Grey could tell they worshipped *The New York Times* on Sunday mornings or went to the Presbyterian church. One of Mother Grey's secret dreams after she became the vicar of St. Bede's was of evangelizing some wealthy family who would subsidize her work with the poor. She felt that the idea was corrupt; nevertheless, here it was again.

"This is Lavinia Grey. I'm calling about your ad for a lost dog," Mother Grey said. "I found a dog that more or less fits his description."

"You found a Petit Basset Griffon de Vendimes?" said the woman.

"My veterinarian thinks so," said Mother Grey. "But I've had him for a while. When did you lose him?"

"It happened while my husband and I were in London," the woman said. "We got back only last week. A friend of my husband was house-sitting, and it seems that he . . . the dog just got away from him one day and went into the woods."

"How long ago, do you think?" said Mother Grey. She found herself beginning to hope that the timing would be wrong, and that Towser wouldn't be their dog at all. Could it be she was becoming fond of him?

"Two and a half months," the woman said. That, thought Mother Grey, would have been plenty of time for the likes of Rex Perskie to pick up a little dog, treat him cruelly, and throw him back out on the street to get run over by a truck. Prince, Towser, and Hercules were probably all one dog.

"Zalman," the woman went on, her voice quivering somewhat as she pronounced the name, "Zalman told me he advertised in the local papers. He said that nobody answered the ads."

"Zalman was the house-sitter?"

"An old friend of my husband's," the woman said. The tone of her voice conveyed to Mother Grey the impression that the woman was not fond of her husband's old friend.

"It was only five weeks ago when I found this dog," said Mother Grey. "I think I should tell you that when I found him, he was injured. His leg still isn't right."

"Oh. Well, we will be happy to reimburse you for any medical expenses, if the dog turns out to be ours."

"That's no problem," said Mother Grey. (Actually, money was always something of a problem. But should she take money from these people? Ideally, of course, when she met them and explained about St. Bede's, they would join the church and wholeheartedly support its work, perhaps even tithe. But take money from strangers? No, she couldn't bring herself to do it.) "Expenses are no problem at all," she lied. "I just wanted to prepare you. This dog has been through a lot."

The woman took an audible breath, absorbing the bad news. "I see," she said. "How shall we do this, then? Do you want us to come and see the dog you have, or would you rather bring him here?"

"Where are you?" said Mother Grey. The telephone exchange was not that of Fishersville.

"Marston's Corner," the woman said. "It isn't anyplace, really, but they used to have a post office here. It's out in the country."

"I'm in Fishersville," said Mother Grey, "but I'd like to take a ride in the country. It's a good day for a drive." The woman gave Mother Grey directions to her house and also her name, which was Ann Souder. Marston's Corner was up the hill and several miles beyond the bend in the road.

Not knowing how these people might receive her, bringing them a broken dog, Mother Grey wore her clerical collar. Maybe they would want to sue her. She spiffed the dog up, too, crooning softly to him as she brushed his coat. When she was through, he still looked like a mutt. Worth money? A hundred-dollar reward? It seemed so unlikely. She led him out the back door and put him in the car. He liked going for rides.

The wispy fog of the early morning had lifted. Driving up the hill, Mother Grey caught a glimpse of the town in her rearview mirror, the little houses, the church spires, the glistening river.

The year had reached that shimmering place where every kind of plant assumed a different color, gold or red or brown, and stood out in crisp distinction from its neighbors. Grasses lining the roadway, their fat seed-heads nodding, glowed a delicate gold. Bushes that in summertime had blended into the undifferentiated mass of green now blazed forth to define themselves. This, perhaps, was how it would be on the last day; not so much that the sheep would be separated from the goats, but that each individual would be allowed to shine forth in his own kind of glory.

Beyond the curve at the top of the hill, flat fields stretched away eastward, acre upon acre of brown furrows where corn grew in summer. In the middle of the last big field stood the church of the Fishersville Assembly of God, a huge tin and cinderblock structure like an airplane hangar. Services were just letting out; the congregants streamed from the parking lot. So many people attending church. Maybe that was what she needed at St. Bede's: a parking lot.

As the woman had said, the turnoff was a mile past the Assembly of God. Struggling up a long dirt road, Mother Grey began to worry about her car. Maybe the fuel pump needed attention. Or the carburetor. Something. But then all of a sudden there were the crossroads, the little stone bridge, and the house.

It was back among the trees, pale gray stucco with rounded corners and portholes for windows. The Souders had not planted small round shrubs to match the windows, thank goodness, but had left the yard a little wild. Forsythia bushes, leafless now, rampaged here and there, and a neat bed of yellow chrysanthemums marched up the driveway. Beside the front step lay a large net bag of bulbs, tulips maybe, or daffodils.

Nothing about this place suggested that the owners were dog breeders, no sign identified it as a kennel, no outbuildings existed that might have housed dogs. Towser/Prince/Hercules must have been a household pet.

A slim woman emerged from behind the forsythia, dressed in jeans and a heavy sweatshirt, and waved a trowel at Mother Grey.

"Hi," she said. "I'm Ann Souder." She saw the clerical collar as Mother Grey got out of the car. "Oh, are you a priest?"

"Yes, indeed. I'm Mother Grey of St. Bede's Episcopal Church in Fishersville." *I see that you haven't been to church today. Maybe you don't have a church. The Episcopal Church welcomes you.*

"I was so sorry to hear about your bishop."

"It was a shock to all of us," said Mother Grey.

The dog scrambled out of the backseat. He gave a woof of recognition at Ann Souder, but he went to Mother Grey and stood beside her.

"What happened to his leg, exactly?" Ann Souder said.

"We think he was run over by a truck," said Mother Grey.

Ann Souder gazed at the dog for a long moment. Towser looked back at her. Neither made any move to exchange gestures of affection. Ann Souder sighed, perhaps a sigh of old hopes dashed. "We were going to show him," she said at last. "Won't you come in? I can offer you a cup of tea, or a beer. Whatever you'd like."

"A beer would be wonderful," said Mother Grey.

They stepped through the entryway into a large open area with a high ceiling, where big abstract expressionist canvases hung on the white walls and big windows at the back faced a long view across the valley. This was the sort of room that Mother Grey liked, stark but comfortable. Rectories were generally Victorian at best.

A man sat on the stark but comfortable sofa, crouching over a laptop computer on the coffee table. When the women came in, he got to his feet. "I'd like you to meet my husband, Roy," said Ann Souder. "Darling, this is Mother Lavinia Grey. She's found Hercules." Roy Souder was older than his wife, not old enough to be her father but older, gray-haired, balding, pushing fifty.

Mother Grey offered her hand. "I'm Mother Lavinia Grey," she said. Towser rushed up and sniffed him, and then returned to Mother Grey.

"Roy Souder," he said. "So you've found Hercules."

"I'm afraid his show days are over," Ann Souder said.

"Is he actually a show dog?" It seemed so unlikely. The dog gazed up at her, reproachfully, she thought. "Sorry, boy," she muttered, and scratched him behind the ears. "I don't know anything about dogs." Well, of course, she should have known; such a noble animal.

"He took best of breed at the Westminster Kennel Club show," said Roy Souder, "and went on to take a group one. The big stuff would have come later."

"Sit down," Ann Souder invited as she headed for the kitchen. "Let me get you a beer. Would you like one, Roy? Reverend Grey has that little stone church down in Fishersville, remember? The one you thought was closed up."

"You can call me Mother Vinnie," Mother Grey said, and sank into a black leather chair. The dog lay down with his jaw on her instep, sighing. Towser matched the decor here; the rug was the same color as his coat.

"St. Bede's, right? I've been waiting for you people to put that church up for sale," said Roy Souder. "It would make a wonderful antique store."

And your skull would make a really great umbrella stand. "There are no plans to sell St. Bede's," said Mother Grey. "A lot more goes on there than may be apparent from the outside, just passing by. In fact, a surprising amount of God's work is being carried out there, in our outreach programs to the less fortunate. You should come by and see us on Sunday morning. Services are at ten-thirty." Less fortunate? Who was she trying to kid? Dead broke and in the middle of a murder investigation.

"Oh. Oh, of course," he said, realizing at last that he had stepped on her professional toes. There was an awkward silence.

"Is your friend still here?" asked Mother Grey.

"The one who was house-sitting for you?" *The imbecile who let this perfectly excellent dog run away?*

"You mean Zalman Freed," said Souder. "No, he went south. He and some friends of his got hold of a hundred acres of cheap land in Virginia and started another communal farm."

"He founded a commune? Does he do that a lot?"

"Every five years or so," Souder said.

"What happens to them?"

Souder shrugged. "Different things."

Ann Souder appeared with a tray of bottles and glasses. "I understand that Zalman's first commune was closed down by the police," she said.

"Whatever for?" said Mother Grey, accepting a glass of cold Anchor Steam.

Souder chuckled. "That was during Zal's druggie period," he said. "He was trying to raise a couple of marijuana bushes and the wrong people noticed them."

"Oh."

"Lucky for me, I was in 'Nam at the time or they would have got me too. It wasn't anything really bad. A routine bust. Most of them got probation."

"And the one after that, I'm told," Ann Souder said, "they all got together and voted him out."

"No, that was the third one. The second was where his first wife divorced him and the judge gave her the farm."

"Does he raise animals?" asked Mother Grey. *I hope he's better with livestock than he is with dogs.*

"Yep, goats, cows, chickens, the whole nine

yards," Souder said. "Sometimes they even make it pay. I don't like to work that hard, myself. Not anymore." He launched into a long admiring anecdote about Freed and his agricultural efforts.

"He once worked so hard that he died standing up," said Ann Souder, interrupting the story.

"Well, not that, but he once did so many drugs that he had to be hospitalized for six months."

"He once had two wives at the same time."

"He once spent three years without any home at all, wandering from the home of one old college friend to the home of another, staying until he wore out his welcome."

"Sometimes that happens faster than you might think," said Ann Souder.

"He has a grown son by his first wife, living in New York City."

"I think the son is in arbitrage," said Ann Souder. "But enough about Zal. How do you like Fishersville, Mother Grey? Have you been there long?"

"Ten months," said Mother Grey. "I think it's a fine place."

"Yes, wonderful," said Roy Souder. "You know, real estate values have quadrupled in the last fifteen years, although it looks like they're leveling off now. There were some great opportunities. I wish I had taken advantage of them."

"It's a very interesting little town," Ann Souder said.

"There are still opportunities there," Mother Grey said, "but they're opportunities for public service. You know, those spiraling real estate costs have put a lot of people on the street."

The Souders exchanged one of those family looks, a communication unreadable to outsiders. Mother Grey suspected it was not a mutual commitment to rush down to Fishersville and minister to the homeless. Nevertheless, she was considering one more time her dream of luring the wealthy (by her standards, these people were wealthy) into the church.

It was true that the Souders did not appear to be philanthropists, or even Christians in the strictest sense of the world. But should she give it up? No, she ought to take a crack at evangelizing them. She would make a modest pitch for St. Bede's.

"If you're looking for a church . . ." she began.

"We'll be sure to look you up," said Souder. "Listen, Reverend, it's been really nice talking to you."

So much for that. "I guess I'll be going," she said. "Thank you very much for your hospitality." She stood up, with difficulty. The chair was very low, and she had been sitting in the same position for a long time.

Towser/Prince/Hercules stood up too.

"Roy, don't forget the reward," said Mrs. Souder.

A hundred dollars would have been very welcome. Would she swallow her pride and accept it from these heathens? Was hell frozen yet? "Oh, no. No, thank you. That won't be necessary," said

Mother Grey. She went to the door. The dog hobbled along beside her.

At the threshold, Mother Grey paused and turned back. "I wonder," she said. "Would you consider selling this dog to me? I can pay you in installments, fifty dollars a month."

The Souders, standing arm in arm in the archway, looked at the dog, and then at each other. They seemed to have come to one of those wordless understandings that married people are said to experience sometimes. "The dog is yours, Mother Grey," said Souder. "As a gift."

Mother Grey felt suddenly small and mean. "Oh, I couldn't accept such a—"

Roy Souder said with a smile, "It would take more than he's worth just to pay the veterinary bills that would be required to restore his value as a pet."

His value as a pet? "Well, then, thank you very much," she said. They promised to mail her his papers. She opened the door to the backseat of the Nova, and the dog got in, favoring his bad leg slightly, and settled down without a backward glance at the Souders. As far as Mother Grey could tell, Towser had never for one moment entertained the idea of staying behind with them.

But still, it was a magnificent gesture on their part. She was astonished and quite ashamed of herself for denouncing them in her heart as heathens. Of course, they were heathens. Value as a pet, indeed. Half a mile down the road, the dog put a companionable if somewhat smelly head on her shoulder. "We think you have plenty of value as a pet, don't we, Towser?" she murmured, scratching his chops. "Lots of nice value." Not until they were almost home did she begin to meditate on the possibility of more veterinary bills.

That night, Towser got all the way up the stairs and slept on the foot of Mother Grey's bed. Dozing off, she realized there had been a hole in her life ever since the cats died. *But he really must have a bath,* she thought. *Tomorrow.*

10

Dave Dogg came wide awake out of some restless dream. The steam heat was on in his apartment, hissing. He felt hot and so got out of bed, knowing that if he lay there, it would be to stay awake for another hour or more, sweating and thinking. Ever since the days when he was a rookie on the swing shift, working sometimes days, sometimes nights, sleep had been elusive. The irregular hours had broken his internal clock.

Two A.M. He padded into the kitchen, thinking maybe he should get wall-to-wall carpeting or something, it might be better on his feet. Or maybe he should try harder to find his slippers. He wanted coffee, but Mrs. Dogg hadn't raised any morons, you don't drink coffee when you have insomnia. He put up a pot of decaffeinated.

While the coffee maker snorted and burbled, he shoved the socks and newspapers onto the floor and sat down to play a game of Nintendo Football.

It was his boy Ricky's game, but all by himself in the middle of the night it was as close as Dave Dogg could get to having fun.

Dead bishops.

Three days had passed since Bishop Wealle's murder, and if you didn't find the guilty party in the first three days, you generally didn't find him at all. The powers that be would be mighty upset if the cops blew this one.

Dave Dogg put the game on pause and began to consider his roster of suspects. A bunch of holy priests, including the lovely Lavinia Grey, who was not a nun (and a good thing too); a feeb; a neurotic librarian; and a hundred-year-old lady. The crowd from Fishersville were on the list because of the Chamber of Commerce flyer found clutched in Bishop Wealle's dead hand.

Clutched in his dead hand. Was that corny or what? A clue in the grip of death. Normal murder cases didn't have clues, everything was a clue, or nothing was a clue, it was just stuff, and after you found out who did it, you used some of the stuff to convince a jury. And you found out because somebody told you.

But there seemed to be no witnesses here. Nobody saw nothin'. Five hundred people, and nobody saw a damned thing.

The clue of the cocaine, which was the sort of clue that Dave Dogg was used to, turned out to be powdered sugar after all, just as Lavinia Grey had said. So much for his drug deal theory. That left all the other stuff lying around that might be clues or

not, the glasses, the fibers on the drinking fountain, the Chamber of Commerce brochure.

Maybe the brochure was a plant. Suppose somebody had handed the bish a Chamber of Commerce brochure from Fishersville to divert suspicion, and then wrung his neck? Here, take this,
Bish. Gronk! But who? Okay, maybe enemies of
Lavinia Grey.

He thought about the possibility of that cute little woman having enemies. The lady preacher in
her ratty church in the Town That Time Forgot. He
had to confess he'd never met anyone like her.
Most of his women friends either had no ambition
at all other than to make it through next week
without suffering serious grief, or their ambitions
involved putting on a suit every morning, taking
the train to New York, and coming back with a
whole lot of money. Okay, there were a couple of
women on the police force who seemed dedicated
to their work, and they must have known it would
never make them rich. But they were, like, regular
people, people like himself. They weren't . . .
priests.

Why would a woman want to be a priest, anyhow?

Well, why would anybody? Okay, to love God
and serve Him in this world and the next. So one
of these God-lovers or their cronies had murdered
the Bishop of New Jersey and dragged his dead
body into an old storeroom.

Dave Dogg didn't look for a lot of holiness in
churches. He had been brought up in the Roman

Catholic Church, and he understood that although the Church might be of God, it was also (and sometimes primarily) a temporal institution, maybe not as anarchic as a drug cartel, but not what you would call entirely celestial. Priests were human beings. Some of them were intelligent people, too, perfectly capable of dreaming up fancy plots and planting false clues if they wanted somebody out of the way. Subtlety. How he hated subtlety in a case.

This guy Ralph, now. Baby Huey. No subtlety there. All Ralph Voercker would need to do was think that Mother Vinnie was threatened in some way by Bishop Wealle. Which he did seem to think. Too bad he had an alibi.

Or did he? Tomorrow Dave Dogg would go and have a talk with Delight van Buskirk. Not something he was looking forward to. This was a person of great age. He felt nervous about asking her questions. How do you interrogate somebody that old? What if she got upset? What if she took a heart attack and dropped dead? Charges of police brutality. Lawsuits from her heirs. Maybe he could get cute Lavinia Grey to go with him and kind of prepare her. That way he could observe them both, he told himself.

The beeper went off. He called in to the station, and Mary Lou relayed a message that a kid named Wesley Englebrecht had been reported missing by his mother.

"How come I have to hear about this at two o'clock in the morning? Not that I was asleep."

"Missing Persons thought it might be important to the Wealle case. The boy was at that convention when the bishop was murdered. Your case, right, Dave?"

"Right."

She gave him the particulars, the boy's home address, the clothes he was wearing when last seen, a description of the dirt bike he had been riding. "The Old Man said you'd want to get right on it," Mary Lou said. "I think the mayor wants to hear if you find out anything."

"Great." Probably it had nothing to do with anything, just another kid off partying someplace. Still, the mayor wanted to hear all about it.

It was true that the bishop had been a very important man. Even so, they were all important to somebody, right? All the murderees. Julio Garcia, when he got whacked, nobody gave Dave Dogg messages from the mayor's office telling him to get on the stick, and Julio had left five children behind.

The coffee, he noticed, was finished perking. He poured himself a big mug and turned on the scanner, just to find out what was happening in the world of crime. Maybe somewhere they were busting Wesley Englebrecht for driving his dirt bike too fast, or being drunk, or something. That would get rid of at least one annoying complication in the case of the dead bishop.

Dave Dogg was startled to hear on the scanner that all the action was in Fishersville tonight. A big fire, three alarms, two ambulances called in. Holy crow. The fire was on Lavinia Grey's street. He couldn't remember whether the house number was hers. Was she on the odd side or the even side? Had she cleaned up those paint rags like he told her? Ambulances. Somebody hurt? Fishersville was a mere fifteen or twenty minutes away; he could go check it out for himself. He put on his shoes and went to look for his jacket.

Mother Grey woke from a sound sleep to find the dog making an unpleasant fuss in the darkness, whining, woofing, and nipping her toes.

"Back to the kitchen with you," muttered Mother Grey. When she sat up, though, she noticed the smell of smoke, not nice smoke as from a fireplace, but the sort of acrid stench that happens when things are burning that shouldn't be.

The paint rags, she thought. Why hadn't she listened to Detective Dogg? Her downstairs hall must have spontaneously combusted.

Keeping low, she put the palm of her hand against the bedroom door. It felt perfectly cool. The smoky smell was weaker on that side of the room.

She went to the bedroom window, wondering whether she and Towser could safely get out that way, and realized that the smoke was coming from outside. Fire sirens and the loud horns of fire trucks sounded, coming nearer.

Dressing hastily, leaving Towser behind shut in the rectory kitchen, she rushed outdoors.

What was burning was Horace Burkhardt's

apartment house. Smoke billowed from the roof; an evil light flickered in the third-floor windows. One of the town's four fire companies had already turned out. The spotlights on the fire trucks lit up the whole block as the firefighters set to work, some shouting orders, some dragging fire hoses, most wearing masks and air tanks. People in nightclothes streamed from the front door. Two more pumpers and a ladder truck came screaming and honking up to the curb.

A general-alarm fire in Fishersville was like a carnival without the rides. The last time Mother Grey had seen everyone in town together in one place was actually at the High Street Fire Company carnival last September. Now they were here, crowding around the yellow tapes, watching Horace Burkhardt's apartment house burn down. Not everybody was dressed. Flannel nighties hung down below winter coats.

Ralph came out of the crowd in his woolly bathrobe, eating something, accompanied by his friend Dan from the group home. Dan was the nice responsible one, the one who always called her when Ralph swallowed a bottle of pills or acted out in some other unacceptable way, so that Mother Grey could save him, first of all from death, and then from getting kicked out of the halfway house by the private social agency that managed it. "Can we watch from your porch, Mother Vinnie?" asked Ralph.

"Please do," she said.

Then came Phyllis. All Mother Grey's friends

were coming to the rectory for grandstand seats. "So, Vinnie," said Phyllis, "this wretched town is burning down at last."

"No, I think it's just the one house," said Mother Grey. Was the rectory in danger? Was the church? But they both had slate roofs, safe from flying sparks, and in any case the wind was blowing the other way. At least the fire insurance was paid up. For an instant she considered what the Department of Missions might do if the assets of St. Bede's were suddenly converted into a check from the fire insurance company. It didn't bear thinking about.

Jack Kreevitch appeared, in uniform, and herded everyone back away from the building. He put up more yellow tapes. Trucks arrived from yet another fire company, the Falcons, it looked like; one of the trucks was the cherry-picker.

"May we join you?" Sheila Dresner came up on the porch steps, dragging a shivering Jake by the sleeve of his camel-hair coat. "You have the best view in town. This is what small-town life is all about, I keep telling Jake." She was enormously entertained. They sat down on the porch steps and craned their necks. Far up on the aerial platform of the cherry-picker, a lone fireman trained a stream of water down onto the roof of the burning building, where it turned to steam and went roiling up again.

"I should see what I can do for the fire victims," said Mother Grey.

"Victims?" said Jake Dresner. "Was there somebody in there?"

"I don't know," said Mother Grey. "I meant the people who were put out of their homes." There were firemen on the roof now, chopping. The smoke was intense.

"I would never get caught in a fire," said Dan. "I have a plan in case of fire." Dan spent more time than any other boy in the group home planning for contingencies, buttressing himself against a hostile world by the use of his intellect. His hands were raw from washing away pathogenic organisms. He wore his hair down around his shoulders, because you could get AIDS from barber scissors, he told her once. His house would never burn down through any fault of his, since he didn't smoke, first of all, and second of all he always went back to make sure the stove was turned off, sometimes five or six times. But just in case one of his roommates did something stupid, he was ready. He had thought about fires a lot. "I have this rope tied to my bed, see, a big rope with knots in it, and anytime there's a fire, I just throw it out the window . . ."

Phyllis was beginning to shiver. "Why don't you go inside and get warm?" said Mother Grey.

". . . and climb to safety," Dan finished.

"No, thank you," Phyllis said. "I think I'll go home. I've had about all the amusement I can stand for one evening."

"Morning," said Sheila.

"Whatever." She left them. In the street, others

were detaching themselves from the edges of the crowd and heading homeward as the wind picked up.

Then suddenly the men on the roof broke a hole through. Flames shot out from the third-floor windows, and black smoke. For an instant the smoke was so thick that Mother Grey could see nothing on the roof, even though the floodlights from the fire trucks were trained full on it. Then three firemen could be seen retreating to the roof next door as the one on the cherry-picker poured water into the opening. Their yellow slickers were stained with smoke, a dirty gray now, only the reflective strips easily visible in the floodlights.

"I'd better find out who needs shelter," said Mother Grey. Was Horace okay? What about Rex and Saraleigh and their children? She left the rectory porch and began to work her way westward, searching the faces of the crowd. She knew most of the people she saw, by sight if not by name, her neighbors. The fire survivors were nowhere in sight.

Hoses crisscrossed the street now, drawing water from every available hydrant. The smell of smoke was almost unbearable, but the worst of the fire was the sound, an ugly hissing that the burning building itself seemed to be making.

Three doors down from the site of the fire, Mother Grey found Saraleigh Kane in a knot of shivering people, huddled under a sooty blanket with her children.

"Saraleigh," said Mother Grey. "Are you all right?"

All at once above the evil hissing came a sound like firecrackers. Firemen shouted. Someone in the crowd cursed. "Rex and his goddamned bullets," said Saraleigh.

"Did everyone get out? Where is Rex?"

"He's gone," she said, and continued to stare at the flames. They were all staring.

"Gone?" said Mother Grey. "You mean—"

"Run off when he seen what he done."

"Passed out on the sofa with a lighted cigarette," said a man nearby. "Stupid bastard."

Saraleigh's boy gripped his little corner of the blanket and wept silently. His pajamas were too small, the pants at half-mast, the top not meeting to button.

"Maybe we shouldn't stay here," said a woman. "Did they get the gas shut off? Maybe it will explode." But nobody moved.

Mother Grey watched the fire dumbly along with the others, feeling, as though from a far distance, the smoke seep into her clothes and skin. It was high time they got in out of the cold. "Where's Horace Burkhardt?" she said. "Did he get out?"

"Nobody knows," said one of the men. "Sometimes he visits his daughter in Ringoes. If he ain't with her, it looks like he didn't get out. His apartment was on the third floor."

"Oh, no," said Mother Grey. Smoke and flames boiled out of the third-floor windows on every side and out the hole in the roof. "Did anyone call his daughter? What's her name?"

"Neighbors called. There wasn't any answer." *Maybe they slept through the telephone ringing,* thought Mother Grey. Maybe he was in Ringoes. Losing Horace would be a blow. Not only was he dear to her as a friend, Horace was one of her few connections with the real town of Fishersville. When the old people die, you can't find things out anymore.

"Do you people have anyplace to go?" asked Mother Grey, remembering her duty. "Do you all have someplace to spend the night, or does anyone need shelter?"

Everyone there had family or friends in town, except for the Kanes.

"Come with me, then," said Mother Grey. "You can stay at the rectory for a few days until we can get you settled."

Only Ralph and Dan were still on the porch when Mother Grey herded her new guests into the rectory. She found the two of them sitting on the steps gaping at the smoldering building. Mother Grey would have said that the interesting part was over; the flames were gone and the activities of the firemen much less frantic. She almost told the boys to close their mouths. "Ralph and Danny, this is Saraleigh," she said. "They'll be staying with me tonight."

At her approach Ralph tore his eyes from the fire scene and fixed them on Saraleigh's tattoo, where his gaze remained riveted as she went swaying up the steps and into the house. Mother Grey was a little surprised. She had never known him to stare at girls before.

The rectory library (formerly the front bedroom) was also Mother Grey's guest room, because the sofa bed was there. "You and the baby can take the sofa, and we'll put your little boy on the camp cot," she told Saraleigh. "Would you like something to eat before you go to bed?"

"No, I ain't hungry," she said. "Thanks just the same." While Saraleigh soothed the baby to sleep, Mother Grey took the little boy into the bathroom and gave him a bath.

The boy, whose name turned out to be Fred, cleaned up quite nicely. Mother Grey was reminded of the time she gave Towser a bath and discovered that he was not a dark gray dog at all, but white tipped with silver. Fred's hair was as blond as his mother's. In a big T-shirt of Mother Grey's, he was a handsome and appealing child, particularly after he had fallen asleep, which he managed to do on a pile of towels in the corner of the bathroom.

Tomorrow I'll run over to St. Joseph the Worker and beg some clothes for them from the thrift shop, she thought. She carried little Fred to the camp cot she had made up for him in the library. Saraleigh and the baby were asleep.

Outside the window, the fire seemed to be under control at last. The front door of the apartment house stood open, and hose lines led inside; no more smoke came out, even from the third-floor windows. Some of the fire trucks were leaving. Mother Grey opened the library window, thinking to let some fresh air in, but shut it again hastily; there was none to be had. A few firemen, cleaning up the last of it, appeared and reappeared in various windows of the burned-out house, opening windows, waving, shouting things.

The ambulance was parked by the intersection, still waiting to be needed, so Horace Burkhardt had at least not been found inside. Except for the firemen, nearly everyone had gone away. In the wet street below Mother Grey thought she recognized David Dogg talking to Jack Kreevitch. The two were making gestures toward her house. *The law never sleeps,* she thought. Even in the deep night, Dogg was on her track. But she was too sleepy to worry.

Her library smelled like an old train station. Not all of it came from outside; a saucer of cigarette butts rested beside the sofa bed, and Saraleigh herself still reeked of the fire.

So. She smokes in bed, thought Mother Grey. As she tried to wash the smoky smell out of her own face and hands, visions came to her of Father Bingley and the cruel Department of Missions and the use they would make of a fire insurance check. *"Rebuild, Mother Grey? Whatever for? I'm sure this is God's way of telling you to close St. Bede's. We'll just keep this check in Trenton, to further the work of the diocese."*

She said her prayers and fell into bed. Smokers in the house. Thank Heaven for Towser. The dog was better than a smoke alarm. Tomorrow she would clean up the paint rags. It was long past four o'clock. Thank Heaven for Towser, indeed, since Mother Grey had sacrificed the best blanket from her own bed to keep the Kanes warm. *Now Saraleigh will smoke all over it*, she thought. *Damn*.

11

Mother Grey awoke to find that the sun was up and the front doorbell was ringing. In her robe and bunny slippers, she went down to answer it. There stood Detective Dogg with an Acme bag in his arms.

"Morning," he said. He glanced down at her bunny slippers, then tore his gaze away to look her in the face. It was true that with their whiskers and pink noses the slippers undercut the image of authority that she generally strove to project, but after all she didn't ordinarily wear them in public. "I'm sorry," he said. "I thought you'd be up by now, Reverend."

"I was late getting to bed, Detective," she said. "We had some excitement last night. There was a fire across the street, as I guess you know."

"Heard about it on the police radio," he said. "Thought it was your place. I forgot what your address was. Clean up the paint cans yet?"

"Not yet," she said. "Are you here on behalf of the fire inspector?"

"Not exactly. Jack Kreevitch told me about the Kanes. I brought these over so the boy would have something to wear to school today. Hope they fit." He produced a warm-looking jacket, jeans, a T-shirt, sneakers, and socks. "My kid outgrew them."

"Why, thank you," said Mother Grey. "Aren't you kind."

"Also I need a favor."

"Come in. I'll be dressed in a minute. Can I offer you some coffee?"

"You get dressed, Reverend, take your time, and I'll make the coffee, if that's okay."

"Yes, of course. Thank you." She started up the stairs and then added, "Make lots."

Baby Kane could be heard upstairs, awake at last and beginning to howl. *I hope she breast-feeds that infant*, thought Mother Grey. Otherwise breakfast was going to be a problem.

Mother Grey took her shower and came down to the kitchen all fresh and neat to find Detective David Dogg serving a hot breakfast of bacon, eggs, and home fries to the new houseguests. There was a plateful waiting for her. Towser had been fed, and a bottle of formula for the baby had come from somewhere, probably the Acme bag.

"This is wonderful," said Mother Grey. "Thank you, Detective Dogg."

"Why don't you call me Dave?" he said. He even remembered how she took her coffee.

Saraleigh Kane ate her breakfast in sullen silence, balancing the baby on one knee. The caftan, the only garment Mother Grey owned that would come anywhere near covering her, was straining at the seams. Little Fred looked thinner than ever in the slightly oversize clothes of Dave Dogg's boy, but he was full of chat. He said that he and Prince were friends, but this wasn't Princie, it was some other dog (with a nervous glance at his mother), and he was in first grade this year, he could write his name but not in cursive. Could he have some more home fries?

"Sure, sport," said Dogg. "Here you go." He filled up the boy's plate again, and Fred ate them so fast that it seemed miraculous that he didn't choke on them.

"Think I never fed you," Saraleigh muttered. Actually, Mother Grey was indeed thinking that she never fed him. She didn't like Saraleigh, Mother Grey had to confess in her heart of hearts. *We are commanded to love our neighbor, but it isn't always possible to like him.* For one thing, those kids were in a much shabbier state than they needed to be, when St. Joseph the Worker ran a perfectly good thrift store right down the street. *Snob*, Mother Grey accused herself. *Bad Christian. You just don't like her because she's lower class.* But, no, no, that wasn't it at all. There was something basically off-putting about Saraleigh, quite apart from her lack of education and prospects. Something unpleasant. And now she was living here.

"What time does school start?" said David Dogg.

"About ten minutes," said Saraleigh. "Better get going, Freddie. You're gonna be late."

He put on the jacket. It was only a bit too big. "Where's my backpack with the homework?"

"Burned up, I guess."

"Oh," said the boy. "Right." His face fell. "All my stuff burned up." Then, brightening, "I can tell Mrs. Murphy my homework burned up." This idea so charmed him that he danced out the front door, singing, "My homework burned up, my homework burned up," and headed for school.

"It's wonderful how resilient young people can be," said Mother Grey.

"Yeah. Where's your TV?" said Saraleigh.

"There isn't any," said Mother Grey.

"No TV? How come?"

"Don't want one," she said. "There are always better things to do, or other needs to spend my money on."

"Oh," said Saraleigh. "Hm. Got a cigarette?"

"I don't smoke," said Mother Grey.

"You got one?" said Saraleigh to David Dogg.

"Sorry, Saraleigh, I gave it up a couple of years ago."

"It isn't really good for you, you know," said Mother Grey, though she didn't believe that Saraleigh Kane would pay her any heed.

"I could really use a cigarette."

"They say it's not good for babies, either, to smoke around them," Mother Grey added.

Saraleigh gave her a baleful look and flounced up the stairs with the baby.

Detective Dogg said, "How long are they going to stay with you?"

"Not very long, I hope," said Mother Grey. "I think we're going to get on each other's nerves." She got up and began to tidy the dishes. "I have to talk to the county social service agency today about finding a place for them. Fred is sweet."

"Yeah, he seems like a good kid."

"How old is your son?"

"Twelve. He lives with his mother, though."

"I'm sorry."

"That's okay. It happens. Not everybody can take being married to a cop. Can I use your phone?"

"Go ahead," she said. "Is that the favor you wanted to ask?"

"No. No, this is another thing. I have to call in and see whether a missing kid turned up yet. One of those kids at the convention."

"One of the pages?"

"I don't know if he was a page. He gave a speech."

"Wesley Englebrecht," said Mother Grey.

"Right. His mother reported him missing last night, and they want me to handle it because they figure there might be some sort of connection to the bishop."

"What sort of connection?"

"He maybe killed the bishop and ran away, or

he saw who did it and ran away, or he saw something and as a result something happened to him."

"How old is he?" asked Mother Grey.

"Seventeen. Good age to get in a lot of trouble. My guess is, he got drunk and went to Seaside to pick up girls. That's what I would have done at his age."

"It's a little cold for Seaside. Don't tell me that's what you would have done if you'd witnessed a murder."

"Or not witnessed a murder. No excuse needed."

"I see. You were a wild youth."

"Definitely," he said. "It's where I first got familiar with law enforcement. Is the phone in there?"

"The living room," she said. "Second packing crate from the end."

When he returned from making a short phone call, Dave Dogg revealed that the favor he really wanted involved her taking him up the hill to Delight van Buskirk's house and introducing him to the old lady, so that he could ask her a few questions.

It seemed like such a strange request that she agreed at once.

"But won't it be kind of awkward?" she said. "What if Mrs. van Buskirk wants to say something incriminating about me, and there I am sitting right at your elbow?"

He sighed. "I think you're safe enough, Mother Grey. Fact is, I've talked to everyone in town about you, and they all agree that you're a candidate for sainthood."

"Ah. You talked to Jack Kreevitch about me. He's a very nice man, you know. I've done a few favors for him."

"And others. The only one who made me any kind of suspicious of you was your friend Ralph."

"Ralph?"

"He went on for half an hour about what a good thing it was for you that the bishop was dead."

"My word. Perhaps you misunderstood him." *What in the world could he have said?*

A knock at the door, the dog barked once, and there was Ralph himself with a big bag of clothing. "I got this stuff at St. Joseph's thrift store for Saraleigh and the kids. Hope it's the right size; the lady gave it to me for nothing." His voice trailed off as his eye traveled past Mother Grey's shoulder to the kitchen door, where Dave Dogg was clearly visible taking his ease at the breakfast table. "What's he doing here?" said Ralph.

"Police business," said Mother Grey. "Come on in and have some coffee, Ralph."

"No, I gotta go," he said, handing her the bag. "Just give this to Saraleigh. You probably want to be alone with Detective Dogg, anyhow."

"What makes you think I want to be alone with Detective Dogg?" He made no reply but shuffled off down the street, trying to look nonchalant.

It was very nice of him to bring clothes to the Kanes, an uncharacteristically selfless gesture. Ralph had come a long way since the night she talked him off the wing dam. *The Lord has done a great work in that man,* she reflected.

But he was still very strange. Alone with Detective Dogg. She could hear the baby howling again, its voice reverberating in the cavernous rectory. *If they stay here for any length of time, there will have to be rugs,* she thought, *and perhaps also upholstered furniture and draperies on the windows, to deaden the sound.* She feared that much time would pass before she could manage to be alone with Dave Dogg or anyone else. She carried the clothes upstairs and gave them to Saraleigh.

"Ralph Voercker brought these over," she said. Saraleigh's reply was inaudible over the cries of the baby, but Mother Grey was almost sure she had said, "Thanks." It was gratifying.

In the meantime, Detective Dave Dogg, relentless defender of justice, washed up the breakfast dishes and put them to dry in the drainer.

12

Alone with Detective Dogg, Mother Grey drove up the hill to the old van Buskirk farmhouse, figuring that it would be easier to drive him than to direct him. For his part, the detective seemed to believe sincerely that Mrs. van Buskirk would collapse from fright at the sight of a police car.

"She's a lot tougher than you think," said Mother Grey. "You don't get to be ninety-two, you know, by habitually fainting at the sight of strange men."

"Is that all she is?" he said. "They told me she was a hundred." Imagine being afraid of old ladies.

Delight van Buskirk's grandson must have done the yard for her. The house and grounds were looking neat and well kept and quite out of place in the midst of Fisher's Pointe Condominiums. The developer called the condos of Fisher's Pointe "Victorian Towne-Homes," by which he evidently meant gray-painted row houses with garish white trim and curiously impractical-looking clapboard chimneys. The van Buskirk house, an authentic farmhouse of the early Victorian period, caused the surrounding "Towne-Homes" to look tawdry, modern, and cheap.

"All this used to be her father's cow pasture," said Mother Grey.

"How long ago was that?"

"Not that long ago. I mean, the cows were gone long before my time, but the Fisher's Pointe Condos went up just last year. Imagine, they want two hundred and fifty thousand dollars for each unit."

"I believe it. But not that many of them are occupied, it looks like."

It was true. Real estate was not as hot an item as it had been in recent years. With luck, the bottom would fall out so far that it would no longer be worth the diocese's while to sell St. Bede's.

Mrs. van Buskirk appeared at the door and invited them into her kitchen, where she was making strawberry jam, of all things.

"My word," said Mother Grey. "In November?"

"My granddaughter brings me the berries in June, and I freeze them," Mrs. van Buskirk said. "Then I make them into jam as I get to it. I always think homemade jam tastes better when it's fresh, don't you?"

"I wouldn't know," said Dave Dogg wistfully.

"And it's much nicer to boil jars in the kitchen when it's cold out, don't you think? The way we used to do it in the old ways was awfully hot. I'm very happy to have my freezer."

"Mrs. van Buskirk, this is David Dogg. He's a police detective from Trenton, and he has some questions he needs to ask you."

"How do you do, Detective? Won't you sit down? We'll have some bread and jam. I'll put on the teakettle. You are allowed, aren't you, to eat jam while on duty?"

"Far as I know," said Dave Dogg. "Nobody ever told me different." It would have been hard to resist the pungent smell of boiling strawberries. They sat at the old pine table. The view from the kitchen window, framed in blue-and-white-checkered curtains, must have been very fine before the condos went up. In the spaces between the ugly buildings Mother Grey could see bits of the town of Fishersville below, the church spires, the wing dam, and the rolling hills of Pennsylvania across the river.

"This is from Fleet's bakery," said Mrs. van Buskirk, plunking down a robust loaf of white bread. "I'd like to say I made it myself, but the fact is I've never been a baker. My sister Caroline, rest her soul, used to bake twice a week."

"Mrs. van Buskirk raised five children in this house," said Mother Grey. (It was true that none of them were members of St. Bede's any longer, but their lives and characters apart from that were irreproachable.)

"Yes," the old lady said. "It was a true family farm. We had to work very hard, though. Caroline owned it all, did you know that? Since she was the eldest and never married, Father left it all to her, so that she would have a little something."

"Mrs. van Buskirk," said Detective Dogg, buttering a fat slice of bread, "did you ever know Bishop Wealle?"

"Certainly," she said. She rinsed out the teapot with boiling hot water, dropped three tea bags in it, and filled it up. Then she set out three bone china cups of different flowery patterns. "Certainly I knew the bishop. He confirmed my youngest grandson last year."

"What was he like?" Dave Dogg said.

"He was a tall man with a bald head and a big gray mustache. He had an elegant speaking voice."

"Did you know him at all personally?"

"No." The old lady washed her hands at the sink and sat down at the table with them, pulling her knitting out of the bag that hung over the back of her chair. "And do you know," she said, "she left it all to the church."

"The church! Your sister left the farm to St. Bede's?" said Mother Grey. A fortune in real estate? How was it that she had not heard of this? Where was the money?

"No, she left it to the diocese," said Mrs. van Buskirk. "I'm allowed to live in this house on trust, but it reverts to the Diocese of New Jersey when I'm gone. She wouldn't leave it to St. Bede's because she blamed Father Clentch when they stopped using the 1928 prayer book. 'Lightie,' she said to me, 'it isn't like church anymore.' Well, it isn't, but after all you have to move with the times. I don't know what she would say about Fisher's Pointe Condos, poor dear. I think she had some idea that they would make the farm into an old ladies' home.''

"She must be turning over in her grave," said Dave Dogg.

A fortune in real estate, and the diocese got it all. Mother Grey was appalled; the things she could have done for St. Bede's with that money. "The diocese must have turned right around and sold it to the developers," she said.

"Oh, yes," said Delight van Buskirk. "Bishop Wealle did that." She cast a bitter glance out the window at her spoiled view and then turned her attention to her knitting. It was the same little sweater she had been working on at the convention, on straight needles now instead of circular. There was a lot more of it.

"Nice work," said Mother Grey. "It's one of those top-down patterns, isn't it?"

"Yes, I like those best. There are fewer seams, and I hate to fool with seams, especially now that my eyesight is not what it used to be." She handed the piece to Mother Grey, as though to solicit admiration from a fellow craftsperson. In truth Mother Grey had not knitted so much as a mitten since Stephen's death.

"This was barely started on Friday," said Mother Grey admiringly, "and look how far you've got. You're on the sleeves already."

"Big needles," said the old lady. "Straight stockinette stitch. It works up fast. Of course, I do have to be counting stitches for the increases. It helps if I can concentrate. That was the part I knitted at the convention."

"A simple stitch brings out the beauty of the wool," said Mother Grey. "Such a pretty color." Most likely she couldn't see well enough to do popcorn stitches and cables.

"So there wasn't anything going on at the convention to distract you," Dave Dogg said.

"That does sound silly, doesn't it? But to tell the truth, aside from Bishop Wealle being found dead, nothing much was going on at convention this year."

"Ralph and Phyllis aren't always very stimulating conversationalists," Mother Grey said. Ralph, of course, could go on for hours about himself, but after the first five minutes you had heard everything he had to say, and then you could tune him out without missing anything. Phyllis tended to rattle on about things that were interesting to her, but she had few interests in common with Mrs. van Buskirk.

"Pooh," said Mrs. van Buskirk. "Ralph and Phyllis weren't anywhere around half the time. I was stiff stark alone."

"But surely . . ." said Mother Grey. *Oh, my word, there goes Ralph's alibi.*

"How long would you say they were actually away from their seats?" said Dave Dogg. "Did you happen to notice what time it was when they left the auditorium?"

"A good twenty minutes," she said. "Well, fifteen, anyway. Ralph had to answer a call of nature, and Phyllis wanted to see those vestments with the lace on them that I told you about. The people from England were exhibiting them upstairs."

"They were nice," said Mother Grey. "I'm afraid St. Bede's can't afford anything like that this year."

"What time was that?" said Dave Dogg.

"Just a minute or two after Mother left," said Mrs. van Buskirk. "I hope you're not thinking they rushed off and killed the bishop."

"Do you know of any reason why either of them might want to do that?"

"No," she said.

Then the detective opened his portfolio and produced the Chamber of Commerce flyer, still sealed in its plastic bag. "You had a number of these that you were going to give out at convention, Mrs. van Buskirk," he said.

"Yes, those," she said.

"What did you do with them?"

"I'm afraid I still have them," she said. She reached into her knitting bag and drew them out. "I'm awfully sorry, Mother Grey, but I couldn't find any occasion to give them away."

"That's all right," said Mother Grey. "I didn't do very well with mine either." It had seemed like a good idea at the time.

There was a long silence, broken only by sounds of Dave Dogg buttering a second slice of bread. Mother Grey finished her tea. "I guess we'd better go pretty soon," she said. "I have to get over to the county seat and talk to someone at the housing authority about the Kanes."

"What about the Kanes?" said Mrs. van Buskirk.

"They were burned out last night," said Mother Grey. "Saraleigh and the children are staying with me at the rectory until they find a place."

"Good heavens," said Mrs. van Buskirk. "Those people in the rectory?"

"Now, Mrs. van Buskirk," said Mother Grey. "They had nowhere to sleep."

"Yes, but the Kanes in the rectory. They're Reeker's Hill people."

Mrs. van Buskirk was strting to sound like Granny. *They're so ordinary.* "So Reeker's Hill is the wrong side of the tracks?"

"Reeker's Hill people haven't the least idea how to behave."

"Hard luck and poverty can be a very degrading influence. We are all God's children, Mrs. van Buskirk, and the Kanes are badly in need of help."

The old lady snorted. "I've been hard up for money in my time, too, Mother Grey. I dare say we all have. It never caused us to do the things they do up there."

"It'll be all right. Do you want me to take the linens back to the church when I go?"

"No," said the old lady. "I still have to run the

iron over them. I'll get my granddaughter to give me a lift down the hill this afternoon, and then I can pick up any others that need doing." Mrs. van Buskirk was the entire altar guild now; she still did the altar cloths by hand, in the old tradition. When the purificators wore out, she replaced them with pieces of her family table linens. A dinner napkin cut in four was just the right size; folded in thirds, a quarter-napkin covered the chalice nicely. Mrs. van Buskirk hemmed them herself, taking tiny stitches presumably by feel, since her eyes were no longer good enough to see where the needle was going.

"Thank you," said Mother Grey. "Your jam is wonderful too, Mrs. van Buskirk. I'll see you this afternoon then."

"Thanks for the bread and jam," said Dave Dogg, emerging from deep thought. "It was nice meeting you, Mrs. van Buskirk. We'll see ourselves out." On the way down the gravel walk toward Mother Grey's car, he said, "Interesting," in a low voice meant only for himself.

She drove the detective down the hill in silence. "Drop me at the home for disturbed altar boys, will you?" he said at last, when they reached Main Street. "I want another word with our friend Ralph."

Here it comes, thought Mother Grey, seeing Ralph led away in handcuffs, suffering a breakdown in the jail, hanging himself by his shoelaces. "Ralph is really a fine young man in his way," she said. "He's had some problems, it's true, but I can assure you he could never harm anyone."

"That's okay, don't get all flustered. I just want to ask him a couple of things. Right here will be fine."

She stopped the car by the curb in front of the blue house. One of the boys, or men, she supposed, was sitting on the front steps watching the traffic; it was Danny, the obsessive-compulsive. "Nice fire last night," he called to her. "Thanks for your porch." She smiled somehow and waved to him.

The detective got out of the car. As he went up the steps, she thought, *But Ralph usually wears those Velcro sneakers. He can't possibly hang himself with his shoelaces.* She took some small comfort in this, and commending Ralph to the care of the Lord, she drove back to the rectory.

She went around the block and then had to stop for the light at Main and Bridge streets. The car window was rolled down to let in the smells of autumn. Gradually she became aware of a distant snarling, yapping noise. As she turned the corner and approached St. Bede's, the noise grew louder and resolved itself into the sound of angry human voices. There on the rectory steps stood Saraleigh and Rex, engaged in a screaming and F-word-shouting match. The clothes she was wearing were all a size too small, an astonishing shade of purple, the skirt cut to reveal the tattoo on her thigh. Of course! Ralph had picked out those clothes at the thrift shop.

This time Rex's powers of rhetorical expression

were clearly overmatched. Saraleigh had a greater vocabulary at her command than Mother Grey could possibly have imagined, knowing her usual monosyllables. She stood with hands on hips, tossing her long hair and chastising the father of her children in the most indecent terms, commenting on the size of his private parts, inviting him to modify his diet in unsanitary ways, and accusing him of socially unacceptable activities with his mother. Passersby were staring, neighbors hanging out of their windows. Saraleigh and Rex, in short, were making a shocking scene.

Mother Grey parked the car, jumped out, and charged down on the quarreling couple. *"Be quiet!!"* she said.

They stared at her, jaws agape. There was a moment of stupefied silence.

Then Rex pulled out a cigarette and lit it, and dragged deep, and fell into a fit of coughing.

"You want quiet?" he mumbled. Then he muttered some other things, threats maybe, but Mother Grey couldn't hear what they were. He turned and shambled off down the street, still talking.

"You and Rex seem upset with each other," Mother Grey observed.

"Yeah, he's upset, all right," Saraleigh said. "He wants us to go live with him."

This was surprising news. "Does he have a place to live?"

"Hotel Ford," said Saraleigh, with a nasty laugh.

151

"Where's that?" Mother Grey hadn't heard of a hotel in town.

"Old car up on the hill."

"He wants you to take those children and live in a car in the middle of November?"

"Says he's lonesome. Ain't like there wasn't others up there."

"Others? People are living on that hill in cars?"

Saraleigh gave her the stare again, as though to ask if she was a space alien. *I need an interpreter,* thought Mother Grey. Not only did she and Saraleigh speak different languages, they lived in separate universes.

"Sixty, maybe seventy people," Saraleigh said at last.

"What sort of people?"

She rattled off a list of names, men's names, women's names. When she mentioned three or four with the same last name, Mother Grey said, "You don't mean families?"

"Sure."

"Are there young children living up there in cars?"

"Yeah, a few. . . . How long you lived in Fishersville, anyway, you never heard of Hotel Ford?"

"Where is this place?"

"Up Reeker's Hill Road. No kidding, you never heard of it?"

"I can't even imagine it," Mother Grey said. "Where do they bathe? How do they cook? What do they do for sanitary facilities? Can't these people get help from the county housing authority?"

Saraleigh laughed again. "Not hardly."

"We'll soon see about that," said Mother Grey. "You take care of things here, Saraleigh; I'm going to the county seat to see whether I can't get you some help. And no more screaming in the front yard, please."

"Anything you say," said Saraleigh, and went back inside.

On her way to the housing authority Mother Grey took a tour of Reeker's Hill Road, a track that climbed the wild hillside north of the Fisher's Pointe housing development. Rough and steep, but the view was sensational. Mother Grey wondered why no developer had got hold of this particular piece of real estate and put up a hundred condos, maybe calling it Homelesse Pointe.

It was true that there were no municipal improvements in evidence, no hydrants, no storm drains, no curbs, no paving. Outcroppings of rock between the bits of vegetation seemed to indicate that the whole hill was a lump of basalt; so no septic tanks, since the soil of such terrain would never pass a perk test. And no city sewers. Aside from that, it would be a wonderful place to build.

There were houses. Some of them, a very few, looked quite habitable. Most were like the summer camps of Mother Grey's youth, scarcely appearing to have been winterized at all except for the sheets of plastic stapled to the windows. Wash hung out in the yards. *You hardly see that anymore*, Mother Grey reflected. The washlines were full of the garments of large men who did things in the dirt while wearing overalls. Was that the terrible squalor Delight van Buskirk had warned her about? Washlines? Or maybe it was the chimneys on these little places, ending below the tops of the roofs, crumbled away or never finished properly. That keeps a fire from drawing. Her father had told her that once. The little houses were probably full of smoke.

There were trailers in some of the yards, and broken-down cars, and panel trucks up on blocks. Some showed signs of habitation. Five or six people, grimy men and stocky women with big hair, were having a party in the back of a pickup truck parked in front of a shack. As she watched, they handed around a bottle. When they noticed her passing by, they stopped laughing and watched her uneasily.

The cars were parked at the end of a long dirt road, a hundred yards or so beyond the dead end sign. No one could ever mistake these rusted hulks for working vehicles; the tires of those that still had wheels were dead flat. What they had that made them serviceable were roofs and doors, and some of them windows; what they were used for was dwellings. This was the Hotel Ford.

Mother Grey stopped her car and got out. Hard to tell how many might be living up here. No one was around, but wisps of smoke still rose from the rusted oil drum where the homeless made their fire. Perhaps they were hiding. The sound of a child crying seemed to come from far back in the woods.

The wind was freshening; it whistled in the tree branches and stung her cheeks. Somewhere a crow called. Children in the woods. Why didn't the Housing Authority know of this? When the snow flew, and it wouldn't be long now, Reeker's Hill was going to be a really unpleasant place to live.

13

The Housing Authority offices were in a moribund shopping center on the outskirts of the county seat. At least it was easy to park. The glass door bore a decal of the great seal of the county and led to a mean, grimy little waiting room, where five adults and two children waited in attitudes of despair. A receptionist controlled the traffic flow of the needy. She greeted Mother Grey with the cheerful, confident demeanor of one in the position to give or withhold favors of life and death.

"I need to talk to someone about getting assistance for the homeless in Fishersville," Mother Grey told her.

"Anybody in particular?"

"Large numbers of people, families with children, are living in cars on Reeker's Hill. I want to know what can be done for them."

"For that you'll have to go to Trenton and take it

157

up with your legislator. We aren't authorized or staffed to do outreach here."

"All right. There is one particular family, a mother and her two children. They were burned out of their apartment last night."

"Sign here and have a seat," the receptionist said, indicating a clipboard with a sheet of lined paper. "Someone will see you shortly." Six other names were on the sheet; two had been crossed off. Mother Grey signed her full professional title for what it was worth and had a seat, upholstered crudely in cold orange plastic with poking springs.

People continued to come in, many with appointments, until there were no more places to sit. Babies played on the dirty floor. Mother Grey got up and gave her place to a pregnant woman. As they waited, Mother Grey heard the receptionist field no fewer than ten telephone calls, each one more desperate than the last.

She said things like, "No, I'm afraid we aren't set up to handle emergency housing. If you'll come down and fill out an application, we can . . . I'm sorry to hear that, ma'am. Have you spoken to the police about it? If he did that to you, they should be able to . . . Yes, I agree, you ought to get another place. Our waiting list averages two years. . . . I'm sorry you feel that way. Please let us know if there's anything we can do to help you." And so it went.

At intervals of a half-hour or so, names were called. People went in but they never came out, adding to the sense of mysterious and terrible adventure that accompanied encounters with the bureaucracy. It wasn't like a movie, where you could read the faces of the people who had experienced it already. Was it good? Were you satisfied with the outcome? By the time she actually got to see Myra Stillwater, a pale woman with strange plucked and penciled eyebrows that she must have done herself in a bad light, Mother Grey's hopes of finding assistance for the Kanes were growing dim.

"Sit down, Reverend," she said. "I think I should tell you at the outset that I can't do a thing for these people until Mrs. Kane herself comes in and applies for help."

Another four hours in the orange chair. Was there no way around it? Ms. Stillwater assured her that there was no hope even of getting the process started, much less of bringing it to a successful conclusion, until Saraleigh herself could come in or call to make an appointment. When she did come in, she would have to bring all her papers with her.

"What sort of papers?" said Mother Grey. "My impression was that she'd lost everything in the fire."

"She'll need a statement from the bank."

"The bank?"

"Where she has her account, Reverend Grey. We have to have bank proofs of her financial condition."

"I'm not sure she has an account with a bank."

"Then she'll have to bring in a letter from the bank to that effect."

"Just any bank? That she has no account there?"

"The policies and procedures say bank proofs. Then we'll need birth certificates or citizenship papers, marriage license (if any), original copies only, please, divorce decrees with terms of settlement, three most current proofs of income—"

"I'm not sure she has any income."

"If she's receiving AFDC, we'll need proofs of that; food stamps—"

"Ms. Stillwater, I think everything she had was destroyed in the fire. I can't imagine how she can produce what you're asking for."

"Then she'll have to recreate it. In the meantime, you can take her these forms to fill out. But make sure she gets in touch with us herself." This would set the wheels in motion, she said, and then the county would mail her a notice of the time of her appointment.

"What if there's nowhere to mail it?" said Mother Grey.

"Excuse me?"

"What if someone has no mailing address? How do you reach them with help?"

The caseworker looked at her blankly. "I suppose we deal with that on a per-case basis," she said.

"Well, lucky for Saraleigh, it isn't a problem. You can send her mail to St. Bede's rectory," said Mother Grey. *Imagine trying to deal with homeless people by mail*, she thought.

"You don't mean that she's living with you," said the social worker.

"Why, yes. I do."

"That puts an entirely different complexion on the matter."

"What do you mean?"

"Reverend Grey, if these people are living with you, then they aren't homeless."

"Not homeless?"

"We may not be able to do anything for them at all."

"I've never heard anything so outrageous in all my life," said Mother Grey.

"Reverend Grey, I don't make the rules here, I simply carry them out. The state legislature makes the rules. If you want things done differently, I suggest you take it up with your local representative in Trenton."

"Thank you very much for your trouble, then," said Mother Grey. "I'll have Saraleigh call and make an appointment with you, just in case she might be eligible for some kind of assistance. We'll get these forms back to you as soon as possible."

"And after that," said Myra Stillwater, "if she is eligible, there'll be a two-year wait, minimum."

"I understand. Again, thank you, and you'll certainly be hearing from us," Mother Grey said with her best smile. So she was going to have to go to Trenton, then. Not only that, she was going to have to consult Father Spelving about his work in homeless advocacy, what worked, what didn't, whether they were going to need a lawyer.

The way out of the agency, as Mother Grey had suspected, was through a door in the back, not through the waiting room. She picked up a hamburger at a fast food place on the highway and returned to the rectory. What she meant to do as soon as she got there was badger Saraleigh to get her papers together and telephone Myra Stillwater. Whatever papers there might have been, though, had almost certainly burned up.

When Mother Grey got home, Saraleigh and the children were out somewhere, and the telephone was ringing. It was Dave Dogg.

"I had another question I wanted to ask you," he said.

She said, "Go right ahead."

"I'm still in town," he said. "I'm down here at the police station, and I wanted to know where was a good place to eat in Fishersville."

"Any number of places," she said, somewhat taken aback. Surely Jack Kreevitch could have filled him in on the Fishersville eateries. "The local restaurants get written up in *The New York Times* regularly. Walk down Main Street and take your pick. Rooney's Bar is good."

"Well, I thought you could, like, show me, and I could maybe buy you dinner."

"Detective Dogg, are you asking me out?"

"Yeah."

"Thank you very much. I'd be delighted."

Mother Grey took a shower and got all dressed up for her date with Dave Dogg. She decided not to wear the clerical collar. Not that everyone in town didn't know who she was, not that she wasn't known even in Rooney's Bar, where she dined once a month with her old roommate and fellow clergyperson Deedee Gilchrist. But no collar tonight. A clean blouse and skirt, high heels and sheer panty hose, a dab of lipstick, even a splash of sandalwood cologne. Just this once, she would abandon the cares of her calling and boogie a little.

A date! Was she ready for this? Dave Dogg picked her up at the door, freshly shaved and smelling of Old Spice, but not, thank goodness, carrying candy or flowers. They walked to the restaurant, passing Horace's burned-out apartment house. The neighborhood still reeked of the fire, probably would for months.

What about Horace? Was he okay? Maybe the police had news of him; maybe Dave had heard something. She asked him: "Did they ever find Horace Burkhardt?"

"Who?"

"The man who owned that apartment house. A friend of mine. They didn't find him in there, did they? Somebody said he might have been staying with his daughter."

"Oh, that old guy. No, he was okay. He came into the police station while I was there having coffee with Jack Kreevitch. Seems he and the daughter went off on a toot to Atlantic City, lucky for him."

"Poor Horace. Do you know whether he was insured?"

163

"I think he was. But he was a very unhappy man just the same."

Mother Grey did not feel unhappy. It was a miracle that everyone had got out alive and well from that terrible fire. It was a miracle that the maple leaves on High Street had turned an almost transparent golden yellow, beautiful in the light of the streetlamp, a miracle the way the fragrant leaves came fluttering down on their heads. Yellow maple leaves covered the sidewalks, and as they walked they kicked them. "I've always liked kicking leaves," she said. Dave Dogg just smiled.

The cuisine at Rooney's Bar, oddly enough, was Northern Italian, and the food was wonderful. It was one of those meals where the entree takes forever to get out of the kitchen, but you don't really mind because the appetizers are so good, the wine is so plentiful, and anyway you're too busy talking to eat. About halfway through the conversation, Mother Grey realized what they were doing. Dave was telling her about his boy, his hobbies, how and when he spent his free time, implying seemingly that he would like to spend it with her. She, for her part, was talking about St. Bede's, what she hoped to accomplish there, the kind of energy and commitment it was going to take, how it would probably absorb her whole life. Still it might be that she could manage to break free next Saturday to go with Dave and his boy Ricky to see the Eagles play football. Maybe they could take Fred. *What am I saying?* she thought. *I hate football.*

She found herself looking at his hands. They

were extremely good hands, broad, strong, and well kept, the nails neither too long nor too short. She remembered with a particular distinctness what it felt like to touch his hands, a warm, sweet sensation, and the memory was so clear that it seemed as though they had just touched, only seconds ago. Funny the sort of thing that sticks in your mind.

They walked back to the rectory in the cold, kicking leaves. He did take her hand and hold it, and it was just as nice as she had thought.

When she went inside, she found Freddy sitting on the stairs in his new striped secondhand pajamas, gazing out through the beveled glass of the front door.

"Aren't you supposed to be in bed?" she said. "Tomorrow's a school day, you know."

"It's not very late. Who was that?"

"Detective Dogg," she said. "We went out to dinner together."

"I saw you kissing," he said.

"Why, yes, Fred," said Mother Grey. "I believe we were in fact kissing."

"Yuck."

14

Mother Grey's office in the back of St. Bede's was quite spare, even by her usual Spartan standards. There were two uncomfortably straight wooden chairs, a large oak desk with a broad surface and many drawers, a desk blotter dating back to the time of Father Clentch and bearing on its margins doodles made by him with a blue ball-point pen (he liked to draw horses), a brass-plated lamp with a semicylindrical green glass shade, and a black rotary dial telephone.

One of the desk drawers accommodated letter-size file folders. Here Mother Grey kept records of the various good works she had started at St. Bede's. She took out an empty file folder and boldly wrote on the tab: Homeless.

It was her hope that this folder would soon be fat, not with the problems of homeless families but with solutions. To that end, she now called Father Arthur Spelving of Holy Assumption in Ocean

Prospect, whose ministry among the homeless was renowned all over the state.

Father Spelving had been written up in *The Star-Ledger*, *The Press of Atlantic City*, and even the Jersey section of the Sunday *New York Times*. It was said that he offered the unfortunates far more than spiritual comfort, but exactly how he put roofs over their heads and got them to turn their lives around was unclear to Mother Grey. Part of his secret, she believed, was that he grappled in some intimate way with the housing bureaucracy. Whatever his techniques were, she had to find out about them right away. Two years with Saraleigh and Rex—!

Father Spelving himself answered the telephone, a change from the usual; ordinarily his secretary handled most of his calls. (Oh, to have a secretary! Or even a clerk.) "Hello, Mother Grey," he said. "What's up?"

She described the problems of the Fishersville homeless to him, in general and in horrifying particular. "In the rectory!" he said. "How in the world are you managing?"

"I need help," said Mother Grey. "I thought the county would be more use than they seem to be able to be. What would you do for these people, if you were in my place?"

"There are some temporary solutions. Do you know about the Interfaith Hospitality Network?" he said.

No, she had never heard of it.

"It's a program where volunteers from various

churches offer temporary shelter to the homeless, on a rotating basis. There may not be anything set up in Fishersville, but there is surely something in a town nearby. I'll give you some numbers to contact."

"That would be wonderful," she said. "It would be best, though, if the Kanes could stay here in town, so as not to interrupt Fred's schooling."

"Then maybe you need to start a local chapter. First thing you need to do is talk to some of the other clergy in Fishersville. Tell you what, though; I have to come up that way today anyway, to see one of my parishioners in your county medical center. Why don't I drop by and give you some pamphlets and paperwork on it? That will give me time to collect some phone numbers for you too."

"Wonderful," she said.

"I'll see you in about an hour."

As she hung up the phone, there was a knock on the door. "Come in," she said. It was Ralph, looking unusually hangdog.

"H'lo, Mother," he said. He shut the door and sat down with a groan on the stiff little chair. His face was so tragic that for a horrible moment Mother Grey thought he had come to confess to the bishop's murder. But he had a manila envelope in his hand, and it was this that he was here about.

"I can't make nothin' of this stuff," he said, producing a fistful of papers. "They want me to fill this out before I can apply for a job at the paper bag factory. I didn't even want to take up your time, I figured you'd want to be with Dave Dogg. I mean, you don't have a lot of time for my problems anymore."

Just what I need. Ralph in a jealous fit. "Ralph," she said, "did you remember to take your medication this morning?"

"What does that have to do with anything?" he said.

"Only that you're being very unreasonable. I've noticed that whenever you're very unreasonable, it's generally a sign that you've forgotten to take your medication."

"Well, yeah, okay. Only I didn't forget. I don't really need that stuff, Mother, I'm perfectly—"

"Ralph, do us both a favor. Take your medication. If you were in your right outlook, you would realize that whoever else I may or may not be friends with, I always have time for you."

"You're not seeing Dave Dogg?"

"Seeing—? Ralph, if I were, it would be my business. Okay?"

"Sure. Sure."

"What did he say to you yesterday?"

"Who?"

"Dave Dogg."

"Say to me? Nothin'."

"I dropped him at your door around ten-thirty. Weren't you home?"

"No, I was over at the factory."

"Well, he's out looking for you. In fact, I think I can safely say that he's more interested in seeing you right now than he is in seeing me. And you need to take your medication before you talk to him, because you're going to need to have your head screwed on right. Okay? He needs to know what you were doing during the time Bishop Wealle was being killed."

"Killed?"

"Now, don't get upset. Everyone needs to account for his time. You know how these things work. He's investigating. That's all. Let me see those papers, and I'll try to help you fill them out."

Ralph spread the papers out on her desk. "He took my best shirt," he complained. "I thought he was gonna get on my case about the cream puffs. Is he investigating you too?"

"Everybody. Even Mrs. van Buskirk. It's his job. So tell me what you're having trouble with, and I'll give you a hand."

But his mind was off on some track, an unruly dog after a rabbit. "Killed, huh? How did they kill him?"

"I'm not certain."

"Stuck a knitting needle in him, maybe. I bet it was Mrs. van B. She didn't like the Bishop very much, did she ever tell you? She thinks he stole her farm." He laughed.

"I'm sure she doesn't think any such thing."

"Are you gonna tell?"

"Tell what?"

"Are you gonna tell Dave Dogg that Mrs. van Buskirk killed the bishop?" Ralph said.

"You're talking nonsense again, Ralph," said Mother Grey. "Do you want to go home right now

and take your meds, or fill out these papers first?"
Was it a knitting needle? She never had found out
from Dave the results of the autopsy. What if the
bishop turned out to have died of a puncture
wound, after all? *This is silly.*

They went over the papers. When her mind was
not occupied with Ralph's forms, unwelcome im-
ages came to her: Delight van Buskirk creeping
down the polished marble steps, stealing across
the ceramic tile floor of the lower lobby of the War
Memorial Auditorium, her orthopedic shoes softly
squeaking, the deadly knitting needle clutched in
her upraised arthritic hand. *She finds the bishop
defenseless; he suspects nothing; marshaling all her
strength she drives the fatal number ten into some
vital organ.* But aren't the number tens awfully
blunt for that sort of work? It would be like trying
to hang yourself with a Velcro sneaker strap.

Ralph was having trouble remembering certain
of the necessary dates. In some cases there were
telling gaps, times when he had been institutional-
ized. But by the time the two of them had worked
it over, the job application presented the picture of
an almost normal candidate for employment, certainly well enough qualified for the mail room of
the bag factory. Mother Grey offered herself and
Mrs. van Buskirk as references. Ralph seemed
pleased but still somewhat distraught in his manner.

"Go home and take your pills," she said to him.
"Believe me, you'll feel much better. Good luck,
dear."

There was a small sound in the hall, as of a slight cough or the clearing of someone's throat. Ralph sprang up and threw the door open, revealing the broad tweedy back of the Reverend Canon Arthur Spelving, waiting discreetly outside.

" 'Lo, Father," Ralph muttered. "Talk to you later, Mother Vinnie," and with a hostile glance at Father Spelving he went away. She thought of calling after him to take his pills.

"Is this a bad time?" said Father Spelving.

"No, no. Come in, Father. How long have you been waiting out there?"

"Hardly any time at all," he said. "I brought you these." Out of his briefcase he took a folder full of papers and pamphlets in seven colors and proceeded to spread them out on her desk.

There followed a half-hour interview in which Canon Spelving outlined the ramifications of the homeless problem, legal and social, as he understood them. He displayed an impressive grasp of his subject. What it all boiled down to, as near as Mother Grey could determine, was that unless more jobs opened up, or rents came down, or the government addressed the issue in a truly effective way, things looked bad.

"The thing you have to remember, Mother, is that whatever the social agencies do to address the troubles of the poor and homeless is driven by public policy. The laws and regulations that fund these agencies define the problem for them. So that the task of your housing agency, for instance, is to apportion the funds allotted to them for the relief of homelessness, not to house all the homeless.''

"There's a difference?"

"Under the guidelines," he said, "your county agency gets funding to subsidize rents for four hundred and seventy-five needy families. If they can find those families and put roofs over their heads, their job is done. The fact that another five hundred might be on the waiting list this year, and next year another five hundred, is not an important measurement of the agency's success or failure, as far as the legislation goes."

"There's something wrong with that."

"You said it. Why don't you come to Trenton next week and help us talk to the legislators about it?"

"I'm still not sure what to tell them, except that there's a need."

"One thing they can do, and it wouldn't even cost the taxpayers anything, is to reorganize so that the efforts of these public assistance agencies can be more usefully coordinated as far as the distribution of funding is concerned. Do you know that it costs ninety dollars a night to house a homeless person in a motel? The Department of Health and Human Services spends millions doing just that. Imagine how much public housing could be built with that kind of money. But the Department of Community Affairs is in charge of constructing public housing, and they don't have that level of funding at their disposal."

"That's crazy."

"Here's something else that's crazy. A lot of the homeless don't even try to apply for any kind of assistance, because they're afraid that if they come to the attention of the Division of Youth and Family Services, their children will be taken away and put in foster homes."

"Oh, good. We can't give them anywhere to live, so let's take their children away."

"There's another side to that issue too. If these little ones can't get adequate medical and dental care, they can suffer permanent harm. At that point it almost doesn't matter who has them."

We can't shelter them, we can't keep them healthy, so break up their families. "That stinks, Arthur."

"I agree. But these are the tough choices that have to be made. Anyway, look these over; some of it is pending legislation, which we could use your help lobbying for, and some of it is about home-grown temporary solutions. There are approaches that have been tried in other states, too, that you might want to look at."

"Thanks," she said.

"Keep in touch," he said, and got up to leave. "I suppose I'll be seeing you tomorrow."

"At the bishop's funeral," she said. She had almost forgotten. "Indeed, I'll see you there. Thanks very much for your help. I must confess that I find what you've told me somewhat discouraging."

"We have a great task ahead of us, Vinnie," he said. She saw him to the door, wondering for a moment whether he might actually succeed Everett Wealle as bishop. Would she like that? Would Arthur Spelving make a good bishop? (What would it be worth to him? Do you suppose he . . .)

Phyllis was out there in the hallway, with a manila envelope of her own. "Phyllis, come in. I've never seen so much traffic in this office."

Phyllis withdrew a pile of papers from the envelope and dropped them on the blotter among the rest. "These were online," she said. "And here's a list from *The Times* of Trenton of old dates when they ran stories. You can look these up in the big library in town."

Suddenly it seemed a shame to Mother Grey that Phyllis should occupy a twelve-room house all by herself. What she needed was some company. "Phyllis," said Mother Grey, "would you be interested in opening your house to shelter the homeless?"

"Not even remotely," said Phyllis.

"Why not?"

"The economically challenged we have always with us."

"Just thought I'd ask."

"So, Vinnie, you say there's been traffic? Who was here?"

"Just Canon Spelving and Ralph. I hope Ralph isn't going to go off the wall again. It would be a very bad time."

"What's bothering him this time? Did he say?"

"General difficulty dealing with normal ordinary challenges, such as filling out job applications. And then he seems to be all upset because he thinks Detective Dogg and I are an item," said Mother Grey, biting her pencil.

"But you are. Aren't you?"

"I don't think so. I'm a curiosity to him, that's all. A lady priest."

"Vinnie, everyone you meet falls in love with you," said Phyllis. Her tone was hard to read.

What's this? Mother Grey as envied sex object? She had to laugh. "They never say anything, if that's true," she said.

"Well, no, they wouldn't, would they? You're so far out of reach. They all just suffer in silence."

"Well, then, Phyllis, dear," said Mother Grey with some annoyance, "I hope you can manage to suffer in silence, too, because I really don't want to hear any more about Dave Dogg."

Delight van Buskirk arrived just then with her arms full of snowy linens, and Phyllis greeted her and left. *What could possibly be on her mind?* thought Mother Grey, watching her go down the corridor. She would figure it out later; it was time to deal with the altar guild.

Mrs. van Buskirk announced that she had just come from the Acme. When she had placed the linens on the desk, she untangled her tote bag from her arm and drew out from among the knitting a folded newspaper. "I thought you might not want to miss this," she said. It was one of those tabloids.

Oh, horror, there was Mother Grey on the front page, in full vesture, looking profoundly stupid.

She appeared to be dropping little Henry Wellworth into the font as Rex Perskie shook his fist at her. Fortunately the legend on his shirt was not visible.

The headline over her picture read, "Priestess Involved in Murder." Then there was the cutline:

Social activist Reverend Lavinia H. Grey is confronted by the husband of one of her counseling clients Sunday as she performs her pastoral duties.

There was a story with it, full of vague but sinister innuendo.

"Oh, my soul," she groaned. "Oh, heavens."

"Now, now, dear, it isn't that bad," said Mrs. van Buskirk, patting her shoulder. "At least they didn't out and out accuse you of murdering the bishop."

"I should think not," said Mother Grey. "But my word, this is bad enough. What will the Wellworths say?"

"That nice policeman you brought to see me this morning doesn't think you did it, does he?" Mrs. van Buskirk said. "He's quite smitten with you. Have you noticed?"

"Mrs. van Buskirk. Not you too."

"A blind horse could see it," the old lady insisted, gathering up some of the linens. "You take a good look at him next time you get a chance. See the way he looks at you."

Mother Grey picked up the rest of the linens and

followed Mrs. van Buskirk to the altar guild sacristy to put the clean things away neatly in drawers and on hangers. So the whole world thought Dave Dogg had fallen for her. Well, maybe he had. If so, there could hardly be a worse time for it. "Priestess Involved in Murder," necking on the rectory porch. *I should have had more sense.* And yet there was something so sweet about him.

15

When at last the church linens were sorted out, and Mrs. van Buskirk had collected the soiled things and gone away, Mother Grey decided that the time was right for having a small manageable fit of nerves. She sat down at her desk and put her head in her hands.

There was a tentative knock at the office door, which was open. She raised her head, and there stood Dave Dogg.

Was he smitten? She looked at him closely, but he seemed perfectly normal, as wholesome and everyday as bread.

"You okay?" he said.

"Hello, Dave," she said. "I was just resting my eyes. Come in."

"I thought I might find Ralph Voercker here," he said.

"Ralph is out job-hunting," said Mother Grey.

"Is something wrong?" he said.

She said, "I don't like being in the newspapers,

that's all." She pushed the tabloid toward him. "Have you seen this?"

He looked at it, looked at it again, and started to laugh, until he saw the expression on her face. "Aw, Vinnie, don't take it so hard," he said. "Nobody believes this stuff."

"I hate it, just the same," she said. "They sell these things all over the country."

There was a funny noise.

"My beeper," he said. "Mind if I use the phone?"

"Go right ahead."

The detective dialed a number and identified himself to whoever answered on the other end. They had bad news for him, evidently, for his face grew more and more sober. "The river? Where?" Out came the notebook, while he wrote things down. "How long has he been dead?" More notes. *Dead?* she thought. *Who's dead?* "Yeah, I'll be right there." He hung up the phone. "They found the Englebrecht kid," he said. "Looks like he . . . Jesus."

All the color drained out of his face. He was staring at something in the pile of papers on her desk.

She moved to pick it up, but he grabbed her wrist. "Don't touch it."

Without touching it, she read it out loud:

" 'I saw what you did to the bishop. I thought you might like to make a contribution to my college fund. I'm starting at Harvard next year.' And it's signed Wesley Englebrecht."

"Is there something you want to tell me about this note, Vinnie?"

"Only that I never saw it in my life before."

"Right."

There was a long silence. Detective Dogg looked completely miserable. She felt so sorry for him that she wanted to comfort him, maybe put her arm around him and say, "Really, it's okay, I didn't kill anybody." But then what? After all, it was his job not to believe suspects when they said things like that. "Am I under arrest?" she said finally.

He appeared to pull himself together, donning once again the air of cold professionalism that she found so intimidating. He said, "Maybe you can explain how this got on your desk."

"No," she said. "This office is always locked. Unless I'm here."

"Okay. When were you here lately?"

"From about two o'clock on, except for the time that I was with Mrs. van Buskirk taking care of the linens. Actually, anyone could have come in then."

Detective Dogg put the note between two pieces of paper carefully, without touching it, and slipped it into his portfolio. "Who was here that you know of?"

Everybody, she thought. Not only her three regulars, but Father Arthur Spelving himself. And every one of them bringing papers or some other pile of things where the blackmail note could have been concealed. But why would any of them—? "It

183

had to be some stranger," she said, but even to her it sounded lame.

"Who was here?" he said.

"Ralph was here, and Father Arthur Spelving from Holy Assumption in Ocean Prospect, and Phyllis Wagonner, and after that Mrs. van Buskirk came. Then the office was open while the two of us were in the sacristy putting some things away. It took us ten or fifteen minutes. She left just before you got here."

"Vinnie, I'll be straight with you. This puts you right back at the top of the list of suspects." There was a world of disappointment and pain on his face.

"I can see how that would be so," she said. "But you know, Dave, truly I didn't kill anybody."

He sighed and suddenly resumed the granite mask of professionalism, Dave Dogg the cold upholder of law and order. "You might think about getting a lawyer."

"Thank you," she said, for what she wasn't sure.

"See you around," he said, leaving. They were the last words she was to hear from him for a long time.

What now? Mother Grey considered, briefly, paying some sort of condolence call on Wesley Englebrecht's parents. *But if they think I murdered him*, she thought, *they certainly won't want to see me. It would be in very bad taste to call.* Suddenly she felt as though she had some disgusting and highly contagious disease. *Involved in murder.*

She looked at her picture in the tabloid again,

gaping foolishly out at the world. *Even if I don't get arrested,* she thought, *I'll never be able to show my face in polite company again.* Tomorrow morning was the bishop's funeral. She had to attend it. But with luck there would be such a crowd that no one would notice her.

Dave Dogg really seemed to think now that she had killed the bishop, and that poor boy as well. A lawyer. Was it time to get a lawyer? If only she could find a lawyer somewhere in the county who was skilled at both homeless advocacy and criminal defense. It seemed very unlikely, though, and who would pay the fees?

Back in the rectory, the Kanes were still out. In the cupboard she found three large cans of red beans, some canned tomatoes, and a bag of onions. There was hamburger in the freezer. She would start a pot of chili. She had it in her mind to take it up Reeker's Hill later on to the Hotel Ford, maybe try to win the confidence of the homeless so that she could get them some kind of help. Also she wanted to talk to Rex. Saraleigh and Freddy could have some chili too.

For herself, she wasn't at all hungry, just wretched and miserable. Hoping to lose herself in the orderly cadences of Bach, she retired to her bedroom to work on bowing technique.

After a while she looked up from her music to see a little pale face at the door.

"What are you doing?" asked Freddy.

"I'm playing my cello," she said.

"Can I have a turn?"

Mother Grey's first impulse was to say, "No, go away." But on second thought she wondered what Fred would actually make of the Weaver, an instrument of extraordinary depth and resonance (not to say rarity) that had been commissioned by her grandmother forty years before from the finest luthier in Washington, D.C.; kindling, probably, unless she could supervise him very closely. So she said, "Can you be careful? This is a very special cello. It was made out of one of the original doors to the White House."

"They made this out of a door?" he said.

"Yes, and not just any door. President Lincoln used to go in and out of that door."

"Whoa, dude," said Fred, awestruck.

"Sit down here, and I'll let you hold it."

Fred sat down and immediately grabbed the bow by its hairy part.

"No, no, no," she said. "You must never touch the hairs on a bow." She inspected his hands then, and they were appallingly grubby. It would take all of the resin in Christendom to make the Weaver playable again after it had come under those greasy mitts. "Go wash your hands," she said to him. "Use plenty of soap. And dry them completely. When your hands are nice and clean, I'll let you have a turn, if you are very, very careful."

When he came back, his little paws were spotless. She let him sit down again, and put the cello between his knees.

"Now, take the bow by the wooden part," she said, "and draw it across the strings." She held the

Weaver lightly by the neck while Fred massaged the G string, producing a sound like the bellow of a bull moose in rutting season.

"Whoa," he cried, in transports of bliss, and sawed harder. It was physically painful to hear. Mother Grey began to realize that what little boys liked best was noise, the louder the better.

"Now try this string," she said. "See how softly you can bow it." He did, and then how loud he could make it sound, and after that how fast he could saw back and forth. Then he tried bowing two strings at once. After working the Weaver over for fifteen or twenty minutes in this fashion, he began to approach something almost resembling a musical tone.

Mother Grey was pleased. She had never considered giving music lessons before, but teaching Freddy was oddly satisfying. Perhaps he actually had talent. Perhaps she could take him in hand and make a cellist of him.

But possibly not on the Weaver. When the lesson was over, which is to say when Fred got bored, he sprang up so suddenly that the cello nearly fell over and smashed into historic matchsticks.

"Sorry, Mother Grey," he called, leaping out the door.

The first thing I have to teach him, she reflected, *is a disciplined attitude.* She put the instrument back in its case.

She realized that she actually felt grateful to have the Kanes around, now that she was herself a social pariah. This lasted until she went downstairs and found Saraleigh in the living room, sitting on a packing crate surrounded by saucers of cigarette butts, watching a big color television.

"Where did that come from?" said Mother Grey.

"I rented it," said Saraleigh. "Had to give them your name. They'll put in the cable tomorrow."

"Cable?"

"I only ordered one premium channel. HBO. Figured you wouldn't mind. What's for dinner?"

Mother Grey made her get her own chili.

Since it was getting dark already, Mother Grey took the remaining half-gallon or so of chili up Reeker's Hill to the far-famed Hotel Ford, there to look for the homeless. Homeless people always need hot food. There was just enough light left for her to find her way. When she reached the end of the dirt road, she saw the glow of flames before she saw the people. Flickering orange light shone on the tree trunks and glittered in the glass of the old cars. The fire was in the oil drum. She found some men standing around it warming their hands. The wind whipped the flames. Her ears and fingers were cold enough to hurt; Mother Grey wished she had worn her hat and gloves. Among the men she recognized Pete Norman from the AA. He hailed her cheerfully.

"What're you doing up here, Mother Vinnie? The rectory burn down?"

"No, I thought I'd bring you folks some hot supper. I'm looking for Rex Perskie. Is he here?"

"Not right now. Whatcha got there?"

"Chili."

"Chili! Hot damn. Hey, Mike, go get Annie. She has some bowls."

Ah, bowls. Mother Grey hadn't thought of bowls. "Does anyone have spoons?" she said.

"Yeah, Annie's got spoons too. We got all the comforts of home up here. We even got a stove to warm this up on." He took the pot from her and placed it on a grate over the flaming oil drum. The fire licked his sleeve.

"Be careful, Peter, you'll set yourself on fire," said Mother Grey.

"I seen people set themselves on fire," one of the men remarked.

"Good heavens. Where?"

"Vietnam. We seen 'em all the time. Buddhist monks, they set themselves on fire. We just stood around and laughed at 'em. They was crazy."

"Don't tell Mother Vinnie your war stories, Frank. She don't want to hear that stuff."

Women and children appeared and lined up for the chili. Mother Grey wished she had made more.

Meanwhile, in the rectory of nearby St. Dinarius, Archdeacon Wilfred de Loeb Megrim and Father Rupert Bingley were raising an after-dinner glass of Father Bingley's best Scotch. Bingley was drinking to the closing of St. Bede's.

"Well, Father Bingley, tomorrow we bury the bishop," the archdeacon said.

"And next week," Father Bingley chortled, "we bury Mother Lavinia Grey." He took a healthy swig.

The archdeacon put his glass down untasted. "Really, Bingley, that wasn't called for," he said.

Ah. He had offended the archbishop. "Figuratively speaking, of course," Father Bingley amended. "I would never wish any harm to befall our dear Mother Grey." As he rolled the smoky liquor around on his tongue, he regarded his church, St. Dinarius, through the dining-room window.

Built foursquare of quarried granite, St. Dinarius commanded a view of the entire borough of Rolling Hills. It was the handsomest church that money could have built in the year of our Lord 1958. Its portals were expensively ramped for the handicapped, its grounds lovingly tended by a huge army of gardening women. The site reflected the position of the church in the community. The best people in town attended. And hundreds of others. Eight classes of Sunday school met every week.

And yet. Last year no fewer than three families had left St. Dinarius to motor half an hour every Sunday to All Saints in Princeton, and when Father Bingley cornered one of them and asked her why, she complained that St. Dinarius was graceless. Later he had gone to the church and stared at its appointments. Graceless? It must be the windows. What St. Dinarius needed was the graceful and benevolent angels and saints that were thrown away on the tiny congregation at St. Bede's.

"I must confess that no one will be happier than

I will to see Mother Grey out of that old barn,"
said the archdeacon. "For her own sake, of course.
But you know, the annual heating bill alone would
buy me three secretaries, a fax machine, and a
new computer."

"Yes, I reviewed her budget," Bingley agreed.
"Shocking." It had been almost his first act on
taking office as a member of the Department of
Missions. The waste of resources at St. Bede's was
phenomenal, there was hardly a real Episcopalian
in the entire town of Fishersville and its scummy
environs, and furthermore the windows, pearls before swine, cried out to be removed and placed in
St. Dinarius, where the congregation could afford
to have them properly maintained and looked after.

"And you tell me her congregation has dwindled
to five people," said the archdeacon.

"Three," said Bingley, "and two of them penni-
less."

"Hopefully their pennies are not a consider-
ation," he said with a sigh. "Still, it would be good
to have a little something coming in. Next year
that place would need a new roof, if we were to
keep it open."

"And now comes this business of Mother Grey
being involved in the bishop's death," said Bingley, warming to his topic. "I need hardly tell you
how little this does for the dignity of her position
and the image of the church."

"Father Bingley, if I didn't know better I would
think you were enjoying this."

"Oh, no, no. Poor woman. But you know yourself she'll be happier somewhere else."

"Still, I'm not looking forward to telling her."

"Do you want me to come with you?" said Bingley. The archdeacon planned to request a meeting with Mother Grey and her vestry, the lay governing body of St. Bede's, after church on the following Sunday. If Father Bingley were to go along, it would give him a chance to check out St. Bede's one more time, to see whether there mightn't be something else he could use. They said the pulpit was a handsome old piece. He didn't remember it.

"No. No, that won't be necessary, Father Bingley. I can deal with Mother Grey and her vestry, if any, by myself."

"Mother Grey can be a very stubborn woman."

"Nevertheless."

16

In the undercroft of Trinity Episcopal Cathedral the entire clergy of the Diocese of New Jersey were vesting. Upward of two hundred of them milled about among the rows of tables, shaking out umbrellas, unpacking wet suitcases or garment bags, pulling on cassocks and surplices, adjusting stoles, dragging vestments across the muddy floor. A holy mob scene. It reminded Mother Grey of nothing so much as her college graduation. This commencement, though, had only one graduate, and the life he was expected to commence was far more glorious than anything awaiting the graduates of the University of Michigan.

Bishop Wealle's funeral was to begin with a great procession. Those who were already dressed were trying to find their places in line; others were still arriving. Here came Father Arthur Spelving with his vestments in a chic black Lands' End garment bag. There stood old Father Clentch, an island of calm in the maelstrom of activity, adjusting his famous hairpiece.

Mother Grey gave her own hair a pat and set off toward the head of the line, greeting friends as she bumped into them. She was dressed in a black cassock, ankle-length white surplice (without lace), and a simple white stole.

All clergy who were not canons or bishops were required to wear black and white; a black cassock with a white surplice over it was usual. The cassock was just a long, straight, black cassock, but one's surplice could be hip-length—a style that made Mother Grey look like a choirboy in lipstick —or almost to the floor, in the Anglican style. The most elegant length allowed three inches of cassock to show. Some surplices had lace trimming of various depths; there were different styles of sleeve. Mother Grey had secret yearnings for lace but found it too expensive. Father Rupert Bingley wore lace. It made him look imposing but fat.

The young Turks wore cassock albs.

There was room for free exercise of personal style only in the stoles, which could be of tapestry, hand-embroidered, brocaded, or severely plain, adorned only with a small cross. Father Durnfey wore a burlap stole, or perhaps it was sackcloth, as a sort of political statement, but that's the way he was.

A few unhappy wretches brought the wrong color vestments and (if they were at all sensitive) suffered the pain of being seen incorrectly dressed. It caused Mother Grey to meditate upon the parable of the careless guest who showed up at the wedding without a wedding garment; he was cast into outer darkness, and there was wailing and gnashing of teeth.

Father Spelving was one of a small number of people who could tastefully wear other than black and white to the bishop's funeral, for he was an honorary canon, and all the canons wore purple. The real canons served on the staff of the cathedral, but there were also honorary canons, a title possibly unique to New Jersey, parish priests who had served God and the diocese in some special way. They wore hoods, rather like academic hoods, and the reason for that was this:

Many years ago Bishop Banyard had attempted to bestow honorary doctorates in the College of Love (the College was his own invention) to his most valuable priests, with a hood, a ring, and a certificate, only to be told by the AATS—the American Association of Theological Schools—that the College of Love was not an accredited institution. "Very well," said the bishop, "I'll make them honorary canons." And he did.

Subsequent bishops had appointed more honorary canons, but the custom lapsed under Bishop Wealle's predecessor, and the number of honorary canons was down to twelve or thirteen, of whom Father Spelving was one of the youngest. None were women, for in the time when these appointments were made there were no women priests.

Father Spelving, when he had vested and donned his elegant hood, came and gave Mother

Grey the old arm around the shoulder. He said, "I want you to know, Vinnie, that I don't believe a word of it." Father Spelving had seen the morning *Trentonian*, with its banner headline:

LOCAL PRIESTESS IS BISHOP-KILLER?

The first thing Mother Grey thought when she read the story was that she wished they'd stop calling her a priestess, a heathen sort of title. The next thing was to wonder where they were getting their information. Surely Dave Dogg wouldn't spread such stories, even if he thought they were true. The third thing, and it didn't sink in until Arthur Spelving spoke to her, was that many people would read this story and believe that she was in fact a murderess. She was branded with a stigma far worse than a wrong-colored vestment, none other than the mark of Cain.

Two by two they lined up for the procession, more or less in order of importance, with the deacons first and the Presiding Bishop last. Mother Grey's place was close to the front of the line because she was among the most recent priests to achieve canonical residence in the diocese. Father Spelving moved to the rear with the other canons.

At the last possible moment Deacon Deedee Gilchrist arrived, plump, red-faced, and puffing, her hair soaking wet. Barely vested, she took her place beside Mother Grey. Deedee, too, had seen the morning papers.

"Cheer up, Vinnie," she said. "The worst that can happen is that you'll have a glorious opportunity to minister to the prison population."

The crucifer and torch-bearers, acolytes carrying a cross and candles, took their places at the very front. The organ struck up the strains of an Easter hymn, "Jesus Christ Is Risen Today," and the cathedral choir marched forth.

Singing at the top of her lungs, looking neither to the right nor the left for fear of encountering a hostile stare, Mother Grey followed along. Somewhere in the congregation Ralph and Mrs. van Buskirk were sitting. Mother Grey had driven them from Fishersville. She had been unable to persuade Phyllis Wagonner to come to the bishop's funeral.

"I can't get anyone to cover for me at the library, Vinnie, and honestly I hate funerals anyhow. Personally I want to be privately cremated. If it were a wedding, I'd go," she had said. Mother Grey guessed that Phyllis was avoiding the funeral in order to distance herself from her, because of the stories in the paper, and the idea was depressing. The other two were happy to go. Delight van Buskirk never missed a good funeral, and Ralph was perfectly well pleased to have an excuse not to go back to the paper bag factory and pursue his quest for employment.

Bishop Wealle's closed casket rested at the crossing of the aisles, draped with a gold pall and adorned with a simple arrangement of flowers. The procession went on either side of it and continued toward the chancel, where the canons of the cathedral, the dean, and the bishops found their places. The Presiding Bishop, head of all the bishops in the country, brought up the rear of the procession; his chaplain went before him, carrying his crozier, and behind him came another crucifer and lights.

When the last "Alleluia" had echoed through the cathedral and died away, the Presiding Bishop stepped forward and pronounced the opening words of the burial service in a loud bellow:

"I am the resurrection and the life, saith the Lord; he that believeth in me, though he were dead, yet shall he live; and whosoever liveth and believeth in me shall never die."

Mother Grey had trouble keeping her mind on the service. The Presiding Bishop preached a short sermon praising Everett Wealle's excellent work and expressing confidence that his memory would inspire the Diocese of New Jersey to go forward in the work of Christ. Or perhaps he said something else. Quite frankly, Mother Grey was never sure afterward, because as the bishop preached, her thoughts were elsewhere.

She could no longer escape the conviction that the person who killed the bishop was one of the four who had visited her office the day before. Worse, it seemed to her entirely likely that whoever it was would get away with blaming her for it. Mother Grey would go to trial. Mother Grey would go to jail. If she had ever considered ministering to the imprisoned, it was certainly not as a fellow prisoner. And what would become of St. Bede's?

Still she found it difficult to imagine any of her friends actually strangling the bishop, drowning the blackmailing youth, and then putting the blame on her.

She could see Ralph killing the bishop without any difficulty. Stretching it, she could even imagine him by some remote possibility drowning Wesley Englebrecht. But he would never, never frame Mother Grey for the deed. Unless he was a lot crazier than she thought.

As for Delight van Buskirk, the idea was too silly. First of all, as far as anyone knew, she had never left her auditorium seat during the whole time surrounding the murder. Of course, if Ralph and Phyllis weren't there either, she could have left her seat quite unobserved. But how would she have got down the stairs, killed the bishop, and got up again before anyone noticed, with her arthritic hips and knees? (Was it a puncture wound? Since Dave had stopped speaking to her, there had been no chance to ask him.)

Even if the old lady had shivved the prelate with some implement of needlework, however could she have overpowered a healthy teenager? To say nothing of motive. Very well, there was the great land grab that had resulted in Fisher's Pointe getting built all around her house. But surely Mrs. van Buskirk never truly blamed the bishop for that. Did she?

Then there was Canon Spelving. Did he really have a shot at becoming bishop? Would he strangle a sitting bishop with his own hands in order to clear the way for himself?

And don't forget Phyllis. But Phyllis would have

no reason to kill the bishop. Phyllis had never even been heard to complain about the loss of the 1928 liturgy.

They prayed; they sang; "Let us offer each other the sign of peace," the Presiding Bishop invited. Mother Grey exchanged a comforting hug with Deacon Deedee Gilchrist.

"Peace, Deedee."

"Peace, Vinnie."

But the priest on her right, instead of saying, "Peace be with you," took her hand in his two moist palms, gazed at her with eyes like those of a distempered cocker spaniel, and murmured, "God will forgive you, Mother." After that Mother Grey had to spend almost her entire energy fighting down the urge to run screaming from the cathedral.

The Eucharist was concelebrated by all the bishops, which is to say that the whole lot of them crowded around the altar and said Mass. Luckily none of them had seen *The Trentonian*, or at least none of them thought it worthwhile to suggest that the author of the corpse be refused Communion at the funeral services. Still she seemed to feel eyes on her and hear whispers. When at last the Presiding Bishop had commended the soul of Bishop Wealle to God and blessed the congregation, and Archdeacon Megrim had said, "Let us go forth in the name of Christ," no one responded, "Thanks be to God," with more fervor than Mother Grey.

All the way back down the aisle and out the central portal, they sang "The Strife is O'er, the Battle

Won" as lustily as possible. Mother Grey allowed her eyes to stray for a moment to the congregation, and there they met the blue eyes of Dave Dogg, looking for murderers. He looked away first. There were a few vagrants in the back, and she thought, *Perhaps one of those people is the one.* Could some cunning vagrant have made his way to Fishersville and planted Wesley Englebrecht's blackmail note on her desk? It would have been good to think so, but it seemed so unlikely.

The rain was subsiding to a cold, heavy mist. On either side of the walkway to the hearse the procession formed an honor guard, and down the center the pallbearers carried the casket, with a crucifer going before them, and placed it inside. The doors were closed, the black hearse rolled away, and Bishop Everett Wealle was gone to glory.

17

As the clergy returned to the undercroft to get out of their damp vestments, the word began to go forth that the ladies of the cathedral had put together a lunch, not only for the clergy but also for any other of the mourners who chose to partake of it. Somehow Mother Grey did not want to eat with a large roomful of people who thought she had murdered the bishop.

Dressed at last in her Episcopalian gray skirt and sweater—Dave Dogg had not returned her suit jacket—she found Ralph and Mrs. van Buskirk waiting for her in the nave. "They're having lunch upstairs; do you want to go?" *You don't want to go, do you?*

"Free lunch?" Ralph said. "All *right.* I'm hungry as sin, and there's nothing home in the freezer but a couple of frozen pizzas." Mrs. van Buskirk, for her part, allowed as how she would like to renew acquaintance with some of the ladies. "I think I saw some people I knew," she said.

Kate Gallison

"You two go to the lunch, then," said Mother Grey. "I have work to do at the library. I'll meet you by the car at one-thirty."

The State Library, where microfilm of old newspapers might be read and printed, was a few blocks away, toward the center of town on West State Street. Mother Grey collected her umbrella from the car and set off at a brisk pace, not kicking leaves but stretching her legs out and causing her heart rate to rise. Exercise was what she needed. From time to time she glanced over her shoulder, half expecting to see Dave Dogg or one of his minions puffing along behind. ("Follow that priestess, officer. See if you can get the goods on her.") But no one was visible in the rainy street.

She found the library much changed from the way it had been the last time she was there. Massive renovations seemed to be under way. Nevertheless, she soon located the microfilm and the microfilm readers and proceeded to go methodically down the list of dates that Phyllis Wagonner had given her.

The microfilm reader-printer was tiresome. Watching the pages flip by gave her a headache. The very earliest stories were about the Reverend Everett C. Wealle of Holy Cross Episcopal Church in Pineview, innocuous accounts of church suppers and ground-breakings. Then came a favorable review for the cookbook the late Mrs. Wealle had written. After that a piece on the historic value of Holy Cross in Pineview, together with a picture of Rector Wealle posing on the steps, looking pleased with himself. How young he looked. This was taken before he grew the mustache.

What she seemed to be finding was the chronicle of a moderately distinguished career as a clergy-person in the Episcopal Church. Nothing to motivate a murder. Between a couple of the listed dates (12/15/70 and 9/2/72) she stopped to rest her eyes.

When she looked up again, the words "The Reverend Mr. Wealle of Pineview" leaped out at her. Oddly, the newspaper was not of any of the dates from Phyllis's list. This one must have been left out somehow.

She focused in on the story. It was on page four of *The Times* of Trenton. To her horror Mother Grey saw that it was an account of a drug bust. A Jerry Wealle, the only son of Bishop Wealle, or Father Wealle as he was then, had been arrested along with seven others at a farmhouse in Somerset County for possession of a controlled dangerous substance.

She printed a copy of the story. Possibly it was significant. Drugs. (A hit squad of white-suited Colombian drug lords, storming the diocesan convention to assassinate the bishop. But surely someone would have noticed them.) This was the same son, though, who had died a long time ago. After all these years, what sort of motive—? (A commune of vengeful hippies; the bishop turned them all in, and now, twenty years later . . .)

Seven names were listed, names of people who were arrested with the son, who had known him, who had lived with him at this farmhouse. If only Mother Grey could talk to one or two of them, they might shed light on what sort of person his father had been, what their relationship was like. That it might have a bearing on the bishop's death was remotely possible. Wait a minute. Zalman Freed. Where had she heard that name? The hippie dog-sitter. This must have been his first commune, the one that the police had closed down.

There was no follow-up story, either on Jerry Wealle's arrest or the commune bust—at least, no story that Mother Grey could find by flipping slowly through the microfilm. Perhaps the charges against him had been dropped. Maybe she should try the courthouse and see if the old court records would tell her anything.

Several years after the date of the arrest story, on one of the dates in Phyllis's list, the *Times* carried the boy's obituary. He had been twenty-one years old, it said; no cause of death was mentioned. A year after that, Mrs. Wealle's obituary appeared; no cause of death was given here either, but contributions to the heart fund were invited.

Then Father Wealle was elected bishop co-adjutor of the Diocese of New Jersey, and sometime after that G. P. Mellick Belshaw retired as bishop and Everett Wealle succeeded him. Various stories arose out of his activities in that office. But Mother Grey had copies already of many such stories; Phyllis had collected them by means of her online service. They were not even remotely sinister.

Mother Grey paid the librarian for the microfilm printouts. He gave her a strange look, or so she thought—*killer priestess*—but she ignored it; maybe he had something in his eye. *If this is fame,* she thought, as she went back out in the wet, *they can keep it.*

In the cathedral parking lot she sat in her car, reading over the material she had gathered and waiting for her parishioners to finish partying as the rain drummed on the roof. Was any of it sinister? How about these stories about the fight with the block association in Trenton, when the bishop wanted to put up a high-rise old people's home? But that was years ago, and the block association had won the fight. Why would they kill him? Or this, where the bishop refused to make any comment one way or the other about the Bishop of Newark's controversial best-selling book. Okay, here was a scenario. Bishop Spong had crept down from Newark in disguise and throttled Bishop Wealle because he wouldn't give him a good jacket blurb.

This was a profoundly unsatisfying exercise. Not only was she still clueless, riffling through these pale crackly reproductions of microfilmed newspaper articles, but she was feeling increasingly uneasy. Somehow it all failed to add up to the Everett C. Wealle she had known. So had she really known him? Trying to remember him, all she could call up was his enormous height, his mustache, and his smile, the smile that had always struck her as patronizing.

In any case, quite apart from the dubious question of motive, the blackmail note could only have been put on her desk by one of four people, if not Ralph or Mrs. van Buskirk, then Phyllis, or Canon Arthur Spelving. They weren't Colombian drug lords, kill-crazed hippies, militant historic preservationists, or angry bishops from another diocese. They were her so-called friends.

Time passed. At a quarter to two, Ralph and Mrs. van Buskirk appeared and knocked on her car window.

"Sorry we're late, Mother," said Ralph. "They took their time serving dessert. Want a bite?" Out of his pocket he took a huge Napoleon, creamy and flaky, half-wrapped in a paper napkin.

"No, thank you," said Mother Grey. So he ate it himself.

"Effie Bingley was at the luncheon," said Mrs. van Buskirk. "She had Agnes Trink with her. I haven't seen Agnes since Bishop Gardner's funeral. My soul, she's aged."

Mother Grey was not surprised to hear it, somehow, considering that good Bishop Gardner had gone to his heavenly reward when she was still in nursery school. "Did the ladies of the cathedral give you a nice lunch?" she asked them.

"Wonderful," said the old lady. Evidently it had been an impressive spread, for Mrs. van Buskirk and Ralph rambled on about it the whole time as Mother Grey wrapped herself in her own thoughts and drove them back home.

Her thoughts were not pleasant. It was becoming increasingly difficult to behave normally around these people, although only yesterday, that morning, in fact, they had been her friends. Once the notion took hold of her, it was impossible to shake the idea that one of them had killed two people and was trying to send her to prison for the crime. It was not refutable by logic. And so one by one they paraded in front of her mind's eye, her erstwhile friends, throttling the bishop, beaning him with blunt instruments, sticking him with knitting needles. Since there was no way to tell which one of them it might be, she felt suspicion, hostility, and anger toward all of them equally.

It was ruining her disposition.

When she had unloaded her passengers, Mother Grey headed for the Acme, there to replenish her empty larder. Although she scarcely had any appetite herself, Saraleigh, Fred, and the baby were going to have to be fed, to say nothing of Towser.

A marketing expedition to the Fishersville Acme was a trip back in time. Nothing about the Acme had been changed since 1950, except for the people who worked there and the items being offered for sale. Indeed, the store with its cream-colored facade bearing the blue legend "Acme Super Market" was listed in the national register of historic places.

In the days when the automatic door-opening device was installed, it had been the last word in modern conveniences; now it creaked and clanked, and the door that it opened seemed narrow, half-blocked as it was by stacks of soda cases.

Mother Grey felt like a tugboat docking the *Queen Mary* as she navigated her cart through that portal.

Since part of the Acme experience was to meet everyone you knew, Mother Grey was not surprised to see Officer Jack Kreevitch stocking up on frozen dinners. He hailed her boisterously and asked her whether the rain had stopped.

"No, it's pouring again," she said. "It'll go on all night if it keeps up."

"Naw, not if it keeps up."

"No?"

"If it keeps *up*, then it won't come *down*," he said, and guffawed some. Officer Jack was having his little joke. It was good to be someplace normal, where people didn't act as though she were a murderer. Home at last. Or could it be that Kreevitch hadn't seen the papers?

"I'm glad to see you, Jack," she said. "It's good to see a friendly face. Half the people I know are treating me like a leper."

"What for?"

"There's a rumor around that I murdered the bishop," she told him. "I thought it was in all the newspapers."

"Oh, that," he said. "We just figured if it was you that whacked the old guy, then he must have had it coming. How're you getting along with Saraleigh and the kids? They doing okay?"

"Why . . . why, yes," she said. His faith was breathtaking. Was that really what they were saying in Fishersville? That the bishop had it coming?

"Saraleigh seems to be settling in quite nicely. I'm afraid I may have trouble finding them another place."

"Ain't that the damned truth." Kreevitch laughed. "Saraleigh never had it so good, Mother Vinnie. You're gonna have to burn down the rectory to get her out."

"My word, I hope not," said Mother Grey. "Those poor children have had enough of fires to last them the rest of their lives." Come to think of it, the rectory could catch fire easily enough, what with all those paint rags and Saraleigh herself flinging her awful cigarettes this way and that. Here was a project: Get Saraleigh to stop smoking.

"Tell me, Jack," she said, "do you know of a good way to stop smoking?"

"You smoke, Mother Vinnie?" he said.

"No, I thought to get Saraleigh to give it up."

"Haw! Haw! Good luck on that." Still chuckling, he made his way toward the check-out line. "Have a good one," he said.

Maybe if Saraleigh ate the right foods. Mother Grey rummaged in her store of nutrition facts. Surely there was a diet that discouraged people from smoking, something soothing to the nerves. B vitamins. Warm milk. Maybe she could get Saraleigh to drink warm milk. That would be a beginning.

Mother Grey spotted Phyllis Wagonner's lanky form bent over the meat case. She was attempting to choose among pork chops. *Maybe Phyllis was the one,* she thought, her bad temper returning. "You missed quite a show," Mother Grey said to her.

"Ah. Too bad," said Phyllis.

"Rupert Bingley has never looked better."

"That's not saying a whole lot, is it?"

"Look here, Phyllis," said Mother Grey. "There was a story missing from the list those people gave you."

"Indeed? What story?"

"A story about the bishop's son being arrested for drug possession in 1971."

Phyllis put back the pork chops she had been considering to the meat case and pushed a hank of escaped hair out of her eyes. "Ah, the bishop's son," she said. "Arrested for drugs, was he? I suppose the bishop must have got them to take the story out of the files. Things like that happen more often than you might think, you know; it's a sort of journalistic revisionism."

"So he hushed it up? The poor man must have been embarrassed to death," said Mother Grey. "Of course, he wasn't a bishop yet. But, you know, after I read that story, I had an idea."

"Really?"

"There were other names mentioned of people who were arrested with him at the same home address. There's one of them I think I can get hold of, and maybe get him to talk about the bishop's son, maybe even about the bishop."

"What good will that do?"

"It would give me a handle on his past."

BURY THE BISHOP

"A handle on his past," Phyllis repeated, in a dreamy manner that was extremely irritating.

"Phyllis, I don't know whether you've seen the morning papers, but a boy from the convention was found drowned yesterday, and they're starting to say that I'm responsible for all this."

"You, Vinnie?"

"I'm afraid so. It's getting to be a serious nuisance. I have to do something. I can't just stand around and let it roll over me."

"Can I help in some way?"

Mother Grey searched her face for a sign. Was this a sincere offer from a friend? Was that a smile of friendship, or the cynical leer of a two-faced killer? "Phyllis, dear, you're doing plenty already just by sticking by me when I need a friend. That's all the help I need from you." *The way you stuck by me at the funeral today.*

Phyllis patted her hand. "So what are you going to do?"

"I'm going to go home and see whether I can't contact the man from the commune. Probably he will tell me nothing useful, but at least I'll have the illusion of going forward out of this mess."

"Good idea," said Phyllis. "You say you know how to reach him?"

"I'm not sure," Mother Grey said. "I'll have to see." She did not elaborate on her plan; it seemed to her that Phyllis was waiting breathlessly to see what she meant to do.

This was horrifying. *I must be suffering from PMS,* she thought. *One's friends don't go around*

213

murdering bishops. What Mother Grey needed was
something to eat, followed by a shot of sherry and
a good hot bath, if she could get Saraleigh to carry
away all the panty hose that were left dangling
from the shower rail this morning. How that
young woman could accumulate so much dirty underwear in such a short time, having no clothing
to begin with, was a bigger mystery than who
killed the bishop. Disorder and unpleasantness
just seemed to follow wherever she went. Disorder, unpleasantness, and want.

"What do you think I should feed the Kanes for
the rest of the week?"

"Hamburgers, Twinkies, and soda pop," said
Phyllis. "And please, Vinnie, keep me posted on
the progress of your investigation; maybe there'll
be some way I can help. Be sure and call me if you
find out anything." Back in the meat case, she re-
trieved the chops she had rejected before. "I guess
these'll be fit to eat."

As Phyllis pushed her cart up the aisle, Mother
Grey's eyes followed her. For a tall and willowy
woman she was oddly graceless in the way she
moved. Her big-boned hands, so competent on the
piano, could easily have twisted the bishop's head
right off. But why would she do such a thing? Well,
why would any of them?

Bath, she thought. *Sherry*. She finished her
shopping, meat, vegetables, wholesome fruit, baby
formula, and plenty of milk. She didn't get no frig-
ging cigarettes, as Saraleigh was later to complain, but she compromised and picked up a quan-

tity of sugarless chewing gum. *Dear Lord, please don't let them chew it up and drop it on the rectory's hardwood floors.*

When she got home, she unloaded the bags from the car and forced Saraleigh to help put the groceries away. It took three or four tries. "Saraleigh, I need you to help me put these groceries away. Saraleigh, if you don't stop watching TV right now and give me a hand with these things, they'll spoil, and we'll have nothing to eat next week. Please come here," and so on. It was like dealing with a fifteen-year-old.

What Saraleigh needed was some serious employment. Suddenly the idea came to Mother Grey to train her as an office clerk. Why should the likes of Arthur Spelving and Rupert Bingley be the only ones who had help in the office? There were plenty of chores at St. Bede's that were well within Saraleigh's capabilities.

As the two of them were putting the groceries away, Mother Grey tackled the subject of Saraleigh's future.

"What you need is a job, Saraleigh. Something of your own that will bring in a little money."

"I don't know how to do nothin'," she protested. The very idea was so threatening as to send her fumbling for a cigarette. Then she discovered that there were none to be had.

"I must have forgotten them," said Mother Grey. "Why don't you try some of this chewing gum? I'm told it helps."

The interview went rather badly after that, but

eventually, after Mother Grey had drunk her sherry and taken her bath and Saraleigh had gone out in the rain and begged a cigarette from one of the neighbors, they sat down and resumed the discussion.

"You're still young," said Mother Grey. "There's a whole lot you could learn. Office work, for instance. I could teach you how to clerk in an office. I really need help at St. Bede's, answering phones, filing papers, typing. I can't pay you very much, but it would be something, and then when you got your skills up, you could get a job that would pay better. I could give you a reference."

"What do I do with the baby?"

"Bring her along. Keep her in a playpen. I'm sure I saw a nice used playpen at the thrift shop at St. Joseph the Worker. We'll get that."

They went to the church, putting the sleeping baby in an open desk drawer for the present. Mother Grey explained her filing system, not that there was very much to it. She showed Saraleigh how to work the typewriter. Saraleigh allowed as how it was the same kind as the one she had used in typing class in high school. Greatly encouraged, Mother Grey gave her a sheet of paper to type, just for an exercise. "I ain't done this in a while," said Saraleigh. "I'm kind of rusty."

"Just keep at it," said Mother Grey. "It will come back to you."

The phone rang. "Want me to get that?" said Saraleigh.

"Yes, why don't you? That would be an excellent place to start."

Saraleigh picked up the phone and said, "H'lau? . . . Yeah, just a minute." She handed the receiver to Mother Grey. "He says it's the archdemon."

Ah! The archdeacon! "Good afternoon, Father Megrim."

"Mother Grey. How *are* you?" Worlds of meaning were buried in that phrase. Did he mean, "How are you surviving under your misfortunes?" or "How do you feel, now that you have murdered the bishop?"

"Very well, thank you," she said. "And you?"

"I am quite well. Mother Grey, I wonder if you could spare me some time after church on Sunday. I would like to meet with you and your vestry."

"Certainly, Father. Is there anything in particular—?"

"We'll leave that for the meeting. Until Sunday, then."

"Good-bye." She hung up the phone. A dreadful foreboding seized her. Bingley was making his move, and so soon. How could she counter it, with herself under a cloud of suspicion? She would have to clear her name before Sunday.

"Something wrong?" said Saraleigh.

"Something worrisome, is all. Here, Saraleigh, I have a real job for you." She produced a list of names and numbers from the file drawer. "Call all the vestry members and tell them there's an im-

portant meeting Sunday after church. It shouldn't
take you long; most of them are moved away or
dead."

"Is it the archdemon?"

"Deacon. The archdeacon. The bishop's right-
hand man. He wants to see all of us; evidently he
has some announcement to make. Tell them I'll
call them later to explain more about it, but tell
them to be sure to plan to be there."

"Okay. . . . What's a vestry?"

"It's a sort of committee that carries on the business functions of the church."

"Oh. Right."

"We haven't met in a while. I'm sure I buried
three of those people last summer. But see what
you can do."

"Right."

Leaving her protégée to her labors, Mother Grey
retired to the rectory to pursue her plan for solving
the murders. Used diapers, she noticed, were collecting in odd corners of the house. A sour cigarette smell breathed forth from the living room.
Ah, here was the cause of that: a saucer of cigarette butts tucked under the radiator, where the
fumes would be sure to rise up and disperse
throughout the house every time the heat came on.
I suppose she thought I wouldn't find them.

Housekeeping problems, however, were insignificant. The important thing right now was to
clear her name of the bishop's murder, so that Father Bingley and the Archdemon wouldn't come
and throw her out of St. Bede's. Zalman Freed

would help her. He would know something, and Towser's former owners would know how to reach him.

She called their number, and Ann Souder answered.

Mother Grey began by thanking her effusively for the dog. She had been meaning to write a note, but events had been moving too swiftly, she explained.

Mrs. Souder said she was entirely welcome. It was their pleasure.

"I need to get in touch with Zalman Freed," said Mother Grey. "It's a personal matter. Do you have a telephone number where I can reach him?"

Zalman's new commune was in the hills outside of Charlottesville, Virginia, she said. "Whatever could you possibly want with Zalman?"

"I need to speak with him. Can you give me his number?" said Mother Grey.

"There's no phone there. No phone, no electricity, no shelter. I think they're sleeping in the open, trying to build a house before the winter comes. But he did give us a number where he can be reached, sooner or later, by leaving a message."

Calling the number, Mother Grey found it belonged to a feed store in Wilkins Center. "We don't expect to see Mr. Freed until Saturday," said the man who answered the phone, speaking in a deep country drawl. "I can have him call you then." His Virginia accent sang to her. Nostalgic longing crashed over her like a wave. She hadn't heard those tones since her days at Virginia Theological

Seminary, and she yearned to go and hear them again, to get out of New Jersey. Tears sprang to her eyes.

It has to be PMS. Emotional reactions of this sort were most unlike her. Nevertheless, and quite objectively, she told herself, it was a good time for a road trip. If she waited until Saturday to talk to Freed, it might be too late to save St. Bede's. "Do you know where Mr. Freed lives?" she asked the storekeeper. "Can you tell me how to get there?" *If I take the interstates all the way, Charlottesville can't be more than eight hours from here.*

"The old MacDougall place," he said. He gave her directions, which she carefully wrote down. They seemed clear enough.

She would leave at once. With God's grace she would learn something that would help her. When she got home again, there would be time enough to deal with trivial domestic problems, such as finding the Kanes a place to live and getting rid of the color television.

The wretched television. She put down the phone and stared at it, and it seemed to Mother Grey that the thing stared back. An intolerable presence in the rectory, worse even than the cigarettes and diapers. Even when it was turned off, she could hear it in her imagination, the soap queens moaning, the game show hosts braying, the cars crashing.

She had even read somewhere that television sets were capable of spontaneous combustion in the night; many were the newspaper stories of fires that had started when the color TV burst into flames for no reason. God alone knew what Saraleigh would install in the rectory while Mother Grey was out of town this time.

Once more she called each of the numbers that Father Spelving had given her for aid to the homeless. Once more only answering machines responded.

It was a sign from the Lord. She would surrender to His will and turn St. Bede's over to Saraleigh for a day or two. Because she could not find it in her heart to turn things over to anyone else. All her other associates could be crazed murderers trying to send her to jail. Give one of them the keys to her church, and she could expect the premises to be salted with false clues when she got back, confession notes signed by herself, perhaps, or the severed limbs of corpses. Compared to this, not even the prospect of finding a multimedia entertainment center and seven-piece heavy metal rock band installed in the rectory was particularly disturbing.

Things would be better after the trip. Then she would know, maybe, which one of her erstwhile friends was betraying her, and then she could trust the others. Right now it was time to pack.

The sensible thing to do would be to plan to stay over a day or two, she decided, and clearly that meant camping out. Motels cost more than Mother Grey had to spend. Even the gasoline was going to put a strain on her budget. She gathered the necessary: a change of clothes, backpack, sleeping bag, tent, tiny camp stove and cooking pan, water bottle, packages of dried food, bug repellent, travel soap, collapsible cup, toothbrush, prayer book, Bible, and all her cash, fifty-three dollars and seventy-five cents. With the addition of dried dog food and Towser's bowl, she was ready for anything.

Her clerical collar and priestly accouterments could stay at home; she would wear a turtleneck sweater so as not to call attention to herself. It would be depressing to be hailed by strangers on the road as the killer priestess.

She put the last of her travel supplies in the trunk of the Nova and went to the church to take her leave of Saraleigh. She found her crouched over the typewriter, still brushing up on the touch system.

"Listen, Saraleigh, I'm going to have to go out of town for a day or two. Do you think you might keep an eye on things for me while I'm gone? Spend a few hours at the church, typing and filing and so forth. Take all my phone messages. Someone might call about finding you a permanent place to live."

"Sure, Mother Vinnie. Want me to feed the dog while you're gone?" Saraleigh said.

"No, I thought I'd take him with me."

"Oh. I just thought, in case you wanted me to buy dog food or something. I ain't got no money."

"Oh, of course, dear. Here's twenty dollars in case you or the kids need anything. Don't spend it on cigarettes, though. This would be a wonderful time for you to stop smoking, don't you think?"

Saraleigh opened her mouth and closed it again, and her face became completely unreadable. Mother Grey noticed another tattoo peeping out of the neckline of her shirt. Remarkable the number of women in Fishersville who wore tattoos. This was a little devil. Why a devil, do you suppose? Why not a rose, or a butterfly? Mother Grey liked the one on her thigh better, with its wings and feathers. The weather was too cold to display it. "Take these keys too," Mother Grey said. "This one is for the back door of the rectory, and this is the front, and this is the side door of the church. Be sure to lock up when you aren't inside; sometimes burglars come around."

Saraleigh's eyes grew wide. It was almost as if no one had ever given her the keys to anything before. "Do you think you'll be all right?" asked Mother Grey.

"Yeah. Sure." She pulled herself up a little straighter in the creaking office chair. "Trust me, Mother Vinnie, I'll take care of things for you."

The first thing Saraleigh took care of, as soon as Mother Grey was out of sight, was finding a match, and then a place under the rug where she might stash the remains of her last cigarette so that Mother Grey wouldn't find it. Gum was okay, nice of Mother Grey to think of it, but cigarettes were better. Best of all was two sticks of gum and a cigarette, all at once, in case maybe your breath might offend. She popped the gum in her mouth and chewed until it got smooth and rubbery, then lit up the cigarette and sat back with a satisfied sigh.

This was living. Maybe sometime she would get a real job, like with the state. Rex! Who needed him? With a job and some money of her own, she could tell Rex to go scratch. She could do this work. Filing was a cinch. It was true that she needed practice with the typing.

She was just getting down to it when the phone rang, some joker calling himself Father Bingley. Saraleigh blew him off, told him La Madre didn't have no time for him and anyhow she was out of town until further notice. "I'm in charge," she told him, "if there's anything really important." Jerk hung up. Back to the typing.

Saraleigh was still bent over the old Underwood, hunting and pecking, when Ralph came in.

"Ralphie!" she said. "What can I do for you? Mother Grey left me in charge."

"Left you in charge?"

"Sure. What do you think, I can't run a friggin' church for a couple of days?"

"I don't know, Saraleigh, I don't think you can help me. What I came for was pastoral counseling."

"I can handle that. My friends ast me for advice all the time."

"They do?"

"Only, I need a cigarette first. Could you run over to the deli and get me some Marlboros?"

"I have a half a pack right here. Don't tell Mother Vinnie. She hates for people to smoke."

Saraleigh shrugged. "What Mother Vinnie don't know won't hurt her." The two of them lit up. As they dragged deep and exhaled companionably, the baby stirred in its desk drawer, making little sleeping baby noises.

"So, Ralph. What's on your mind? You got a problem? Sit down and tell me all about it. Don't hold back nothin'."

"I'm depressed," he said.

There wasn't an ashtray, but there was a pencil cup, so she flicked her cigarette into that. "You're depressed. Why are you depressed?"

He sighed. "Well, first of all, I didn't get the job at the paper bag factory."

Saraleigh shook her head. "You don't want to work over there, anyway, Ralph. The pay is shit and they fire your ass after six months because they don't want to pay you no health benefits."

"Really?" he said.

"I knew a guy lost a finger in that factory. It ain't even safe. Trust me, Ralph, you don't want a job there."

"Well . . . um . . . what I'm really depressed about is my wife."

"Your *wife*? Ralphie! You're *married*?" Who would have thought this bozo was married? She had to laugh.

"Well, no . . . not anymore. . . ." He began to tell the long painful story of his marriage—the story was longer than the marriage—and as he droned on, Saraleigh gave him pastoral counseling, which is to say she nodded and said, "Uh-huh, uh-huh," whenever he gave her an opening. After fifteen or twenty minutes the significance of what he had said began to dawn on her.

"So what you're telling me is you ain't been with a woman in a year and a half."

"Uh . . . right."

"Well, Jesus, Ralphie, no wonder you're depressed. You need to get laid."

"Oh."

"Tell you what. Come on over to the rectory later on. We'll see what La Madre left in the freezer, and maybe I'll do a little more pastoral counseling."

"Uh . . . okay."

"See ya." She returned to her typing. It got easier with practice. There was a long cigarette burn on the desk now, but if she pulled the desk blotter over on top of it, Mother Grey would never notice.

18

Do I really believe Zalman Freed will help me? Mother Grey asked herself as the Nova's speedometer edged toward seventy. *Or am I merely running away?* In her mind's eye the front porch of the rectory appeared, and her imagination peopled it with a crowd of her tormentors, Saraleigh and her howling baby, Dave Dogg with his cold accusing eyes, Bingley and the Archdeacon, Rex cursing, and the newspersons of last Sunday's service. And those were only her adversaries. Of her friends, one seemed to be trying to get her prosecuted for murder. Running away was not mere, she decided. It was critical. In another day or two she would have the starch to deal with all these people, but not now.

Through the clear and starry night she drove, pushing the Nova to its uttermost limits (somewhere around sixty-five, when the steering wheel began to shimmy). She tried singing to the dog "Una Voce Poco Fa," bits of Handel's *Messiah*, a selection of gospel songs, a few rousing numbers from the 1982 Hymnal. Towser emitted a great snuffly sigh and went off to sleep. She played her supply of Yo-Yo Ma tapes. The last one ended while she was still in Maryland, and then she had to dip into the Budapest String Quartet. The dog slept the whole time.

She drove until she began to see things on the dark road that weren't there, herds of deer, swarms of bugs, distant tidal waves rolling closer. A fast-food rest stop appeared, and she pulled into the parking lot and napped uncomfortably in the front seat for an hour. Waking suddenly, she struck her head on the door handle and sat up with a sore head and a dull pain in her back.

"Coffee. A little exercise," she thought. "Maybe a danish." Her watch said four-fifteen. Towser snorted and rolled over in his sleep. Quietly she let herself out of the car and locked it.

A brisk lungful of cold air woke her the rest of the way. Frost lay on the grass, twinkling in the inviting light that streamed from the restaurant. Inside, it was warm and smelled of sausage.

A man and a woman sat at the counter, truckers by the look of them, maybe a husband and wife team. They looked alike, dressed from head to foot in blue denim and quilted brown stuff, eating their eggs and sausage almost in unison. Neither said a word.

Mother Grey wondered for a moment what it might be like to have such a relationship, coexisting in cowlike contentment without the necessity for words. She and Stephen had not had time to reach that point; they had talked and talked, right up to the time when he was too sick to talk, and even a little beyond. The closest she had ever come was with her friends, playing chamber music; when it was going well, they were of one mind, perfectly in sympathy, and needed no words.

From somewhere in the back a young waitress appeared, smiling as though it were a secret treat to be up at four in the morning. "What can I get you?" she said.

"Coffee, please," said Mother Grey. "And some . . . oh, I don't know. . . ." Sausage would be good, but it would probably take a while. She looked at the muffins and doughnuts, attractively arranged in a round glass case. No, they would surely be greasy. "What kind of pie do you have?"

"Apple," the waitress said. Mother Grey ordered a slice. It was remarkably good, the crust flaky, the filling not oversweetened. Good southern pie. How far she was from Fishersville. How she would love to get back in the car and keep going, driving and driving for days.

She wondered what Dave Dogg was doing. *Sleeping, of course,* said a nasty little voice in her head. Had events reached such a pass that she was about to start having romantic thoughts about Dave Dogg in lonesome roadside luncheonettes? What foolishness.

She gave the waitress her pint Thermos to fill with fresh coffee, and thus equipped she hit the road again. At six-twenty the sun rose, just in time to light her way off the interstate and into the little village of Wilkins Center. She recognized the feed store from the name on the front of it. Not a soul was in sight.

Mother Grey admitted to herself that she had dared to hope for a diner full of early-morning local people, with fried eggs and sausage and maybe some grits. The image of Ma and Pa Trucker eating their sausages was still in her mind, causing her to feel hunger for more than companionship now. There was nowhere to eat in Wilkins Center, though, not so much as a closed gas station with a snack-vending machine. *Why didn't I buy one of those doughnuts?* A good grease feast would go down very nicely about now. She parked the car anyway and got out to stretch her legs and waggle her shoulders.

Back in the car, she took the directions for the old MacDougall place out of the glove compartment and proceeded onward. All landmarks were as promised, but the driveway—or woods road—that led to the homestead of Freed et al. was so much longer than Mother Grey had anticipated, so much steeper, and so much muddier that she began to fear first of all that she was on the wrong road, and then that the Nova would get stuck in the ditch.

But as the road turned downward and the little valley opened out before her, she saw that this was indeed her destination. A crudely painted sign had been nailed to a tree: PERELANDRA IV. "You can't miss it," as the feed store man had said.

A weathered cowshed stood at the end of the drive, and rolling over the hill beyond it was a fenced green pasture. In the woods to the west the bare frame of a good-size house could be seen among the trees, its rafters catching the pink light of the early morning sun.

Mother Grey pulled off the drive onto a flat hard place that looked like a safe spot to park, set the brake, and turned off the engine. The birds of the Virginia countryside were greeting the new day at the tops of their voices. Somewhere close by, the *clonk, clonk* of a cowbell sounded. The air was sweet and warmer than on the interstate.

As she got out of the car and stretched herself, Mother Grey became aware that another car was coming down the drive. It passed her, slowly—the young woman who was driving gave Mother Grey a merciless once-over—and parked down by the cowshed.

Towser materialized beside Mother Grey's left leg. She clipped on his leash and went down to introduce herself to the young woman, who was standing waiting by the cowshed in high heels and black fishnet stockings.

It was evident from the suspicious way the woman was staring at her that she thought Mother Grey was up to no good. *Maybe she takes me for a county social worker,* she thought. *I should have worn the clerical collar.*

"Good morning," Mother Grey said to her. "I'm Lavinia Grey. I just drove all the way from New Jersey to talk to Zalman Freed."

"Hi. Zal isn't here today; he went to Richmond to get a stove."

"Do you expect him back soon?"

"Maybe this afternoon," she said. She opened the trunk of her car and took out two string bags full of groceries. "What do you want with Zal?" she said. Then, getting a good look at Mother Grey's face, "Hey, wait a minute, aren't you that priest?"

"I'm a priest," Mother Grey admitted. *Killer priestess.* Apparently there were supermarket tabloids everywhere you went.

The girl laughed, apparently with relief. "I thought you were a narc," she said. "I'm sorry. I'm Mazie Smith."

"Lavinia Grey," said Mother Grey.

"What kind of dog is that?"

"He's a Petit Basset Griffon de Vendimes," said Mother Grey. She felt oddly pleased to be able to give Towser a dignified identity.

"Never heard of that one," said Mazie. "Are you hungry? Let me get out of these waitress clothes, and I'll make us some breakfast."

"Can I do anything to help?"

"Do you know how to start a Coleman stove?"

"Certainly." Though she was more used to her little alcohol stove, lighting a gasoline camp stove was well within Mother Grey's capabilities.

There was a lean-to built against the far wall of the cowshed. Mazie pushed aside the blankets that covered the opening and ducked inside, taking her string bags with her. She came out with the stove and a can of gasoline, which she placed on a rude table under the trees. "Do your thing, Lavinia," she said. "Or should I call you Father?"

"You can call me Mother Vinnie if you want." Mazie gave her matches and went back into the lean-to. Mother Grey heard murmured voices and surmised that there were people living in there, although she couldn't tell how many. After Mother Grey had pumped up the stove with the correct degree of pressure to maintain an even flame—it took two or three tries—Mazie reappeared in jeans and muddy work boots, carrying a big blue spatterware percolator loaded up with water and coffee.

"That's the end of the drinking water," said Mazie. "I'll have to go for more."

"Where's your water supply?"

"There's a spring that comes out of a rock at the bottom of the hill over there," she said. "It's right between the two willow trees."

"Let me get it." Mother Grey tied Towser's leash to a sapling, taking no chances of his running away again, and set off over the hill with an empty pail in either hand. A path led straight to the spring. The willows were old, large, and symmetrical, suggesting that they had been planted there many decades ago by human hands. How many people had tried to farm this property, she wondered, in the course of the last three hundred years? It was an interesting archaeological problem. There was no farmhouse to be seen; perhaps it had burned.

She filled the water pails. Later today she would look around to see if there were old foundations. If she was still awake. More likely she would pitch her tent somewhere out of the way and nap until Zalman Freed returned from his errand, for she was feeling very sleepy. It had been years since she had gone an entire night without sleep.

When she came back, the communards were all up and gathered around the stove, three toddlers, two more young women, and two large men dressed in coveralls like stage mountaineers. They gave her fresh coffee with Jersey cow's milk as thick as cream. One of the men scrambled some eggs. It was one of the best breakfasts she had ever eaten, altogether comparable to Dave Dogg's home fries.

They all ate breakfast standing up, except for two of the toddlers, who had high chairs. "The eggs are from our own chickens," Mazie said. The chickens were beginning to be in evidence, wandering underfoot. Mother Grey inquired politely about the various agricultural projects of the commune.

The taller of the men, the one with the hair in his eyes, explained that they raised free-running chickens—or encouraged them to raise themselves—for their organically pure if cholesterol-laden eggs, for which there was a lively market in Charlottesville. They also kept a free-running Jersey cow and her calf. The cow's milk was so rich that they had to discourage the calf from drinking it, because it made him sick. He was given some sort of formula instead.

Their vegetable garden yielded a good crop this year; with the wood stove that Zalman was bringing from his aunt's house in Richmond, they would be able to can a good part of the yield next year. They were trying to finish the house, or at least get it roofed over and sheathed, before the coming of winter.

Although she was curious to know whether they all bunked in the lean-to, Mother Grey tactfully avoided the subject of their sleeping arrangements. On her way to the outhouse she was relieved to observe two large tents, army surplus by the look of them. It must be that the three families had separate quarters.

Then to her horror she discovered that the outhouse had no door.

It was probably private enough, if drafty; the opening where the door should have been faced away from the habitations of the humans and overlooked instead the rolling meadow where the cow was grazing. Still Mother Grey availed herself of the facilities as quickly as possible. Someone might come along, one of the men, perhaps, or a schoolbus-load of children. *Killer priestess dies of embarrassment in rural outhouse.*

She returned to the lean-to and helped Mazie finish up the breakfast dishes while everyone else went to work on the house and the babies played among the nails and shavings. As she put the last dish away, Mazie said, "I'm going to crash."

By the everyday tone in which she made this announcement, Mother Grey understood her to mean something normal, as opposed to something violent; probably she meant she was going to get some sleep. Mother Grey allowed as how she, too, was about ready to crash. She wasn't at all certain, however, whether she meant to go to sleep or to fall forward with her face in the dirt. It had been a very long night.

There was another nice flat place in the woods near where she had parked her car. The ground there was soft enough to get her tent pegs into with only a little steady pressure. The tent went up quickly. Her sleeping bag had never looked so good. After Towser had crawled into the tent, she zipped up the tent opening to keep out any wandering wildlife and wiggled between the slippery layers of Hollofil and rip stop nylon. Towser curled up companionably at her feet.

Birds sang her to sleep. She dreamed of being a Girl Scout; she dreamed that Stephen was alive again; she dreamed about Dave Dogg. It was one of those dreams that seem perfectly lovely while you are dreaming them, but when you waken and realize what it was that you allowed yourself to do in your sleep, you are embarrassed half to death.

19

T owser woke her up, barking. Someone was outside the tent. The light was fading; the birds were singing their clear lovely evening song. She had slept the day away.

"Mother Vinnie, Zal is home," called Mazie. "If you want to see him. I have to go to work now."

"Thank you," said Mother Grey. She crawled out of the tent and stretched herself. There stood Mazie in her waitress outfit with the fishnet stockings. It seemed too cold now for fishnet; deep purple clouds, almost like a storm front, rose up behind the hills in the west and streamed across a lavender sky.

The freshening breeze carried a smell of garlic. Pots of tomato sauce bubbled on the Coleman stove. The sound of hammers and saws still came from the half-built house, although it seemed to Mother Grey that there wasn't enough light left to work by.

Zalman Freed, tall, bearded, slightly stooped,

older than any of the other communards, stood by the side of a battered pickup truck and contemplated a large cast-iron cookstove in the back. It looked very heavy. The weight of the stove appeared to be such that the muscle of the entire commune would be needed just to get it out of the truck.

Mazie went up to him, kissed him on the cheek, and said, "Zal, here's Vinnie. She's been waiting to talk to you. I'm going. 'Bye." She pulled her coat around her and teetered to the car. How she kept from losing those high heels in the mud was a mystery to Mother Grey.

Freed turned his attention to Mother Grey with an expression of polite and pleasant blankness, as though he had no idea who she was. Either he had managed to avoid supermarkets and miss the tabloid headlines, or it was a matter of no interest to him that she might be involved in the death of the Bishop of the Diocese of New Jersey. Good. She shook his hand and introduced herself, but not as a priestess, killer or otherwise.

"I'm Lavinia Grey, Mr. Freed. I'm looking into the death of Jerry Wealle's father. I came here to ask you about Jerry."

"Jerry Wealle," he said dreamily. "Does that name take me back a long way."

"Anything you can tell me would be very helpful."

He glanced at the stove. "Telling you all I know about Jerry Wealle is going to take some time," he said. When he smiled, his face was transformed;

Mother Grey saw the charm that could still attract a crowd of young people to his commune. "Let us get this stove unloaded first, and then you can have dinner with us."

She offered to share her food. "What do you have there?" said Freed.

She examined the aluminum envelopes. "Beef stroganoff and chicken gai ding."

"No thanks, Lavinia. Everybody here is ovo-lacto-vegetarian." Suddenly Towser appeared and began to sniff at Freed's pants. He must have got out of the tent somehow. "Good God, it's Hercules!" said Freed. The dog took a step back, and the two regarded one another with familiarity but without affection. "Where did you come from?"

"He turned up on my doorstep injured," said Mother Grey. "The Souders gave him to me. I call him Towser." She was half expecting the dog to run away again at the sight of Freed, who she imagined had driven him away to begin with, but Towser stood his ground in a dignified manner. She scratched him behind the ear.

"Have you seen the house?" said Freed.

"Not up close."

"Come on, I'll give you a tour." They picked their way through the stones and mud. The closer she got to the skeleton of a house, the bigger it looked, until at last, standing in the middle of what was to be the living room, she said, "It's ambitious."

"We're going to need plenty of room," he said. "My old lady is expecting." He pointed out a pile of rocks in a shaft up the middle of the house and explained in terms that she could never afterward remember that it was to be used for heat somehow; the technology was solar, he said.

She noticed that the sheathing was being applied in a more or less random manner. "Maybe it would be a good idea to get the sheathing put up on the north side first," she said, not wanting to seem critical but thinking of the children.

"Hm," he said. "Do you think so? Winter comes pretty late to these parts. Or so they tell me. We haven't even had a really hard freeze yet."

"Feels kind of cold to me," said Mother Grey. "Of course, that's only my opinion."

"It's something to think about," said Freed. "First we need to get the roof on, though. Tomorrow we're getting the tarpaper. Yo! Men!"

The two other men ceased pounding and banging in the rafters.

"Let's get that stove out of the truck!"

They gathered then for the unloading of the stove, a titanic effort involving all the men and one or two of the women. Mother Grey helped to position the plywood under this behemoth as it came off the truck. It was felt that without the plywood it would sink out of sight in the mud. Mother Grey's private opinion was that it was miraculous that no one was injured in the operation.

They were so delighted with the success of the unloading of the stove that Freed declared it was time to have a party.

Another sheet of plywood was found and put on

sawhorses to make a table. Mother Grey helped to
set it. Zalman Freed sat at the head of the table on
the only real chair, and the others sat on long
benches. Mother Grey was placed at Freed's right.
By the light of an oil lamp they dined on whole-
wheat spaghetti from the health food store in
Charlottesville, with homemade sauce, and other
things that could be boiled on a Coleman camp
stove or eaten raw.

Now that they had an oven, one of the women
said, they could bake bread. Mother Grey imagined that she remembered that bread; it would
have extra wheat germ in it and maybe some bran,
the old food of the serious whole-earth hippies.

There was a bite to the wind that hadn't been
there before the sun went down. Mother Grey's
hands were growing too cold to hold her fork. *At
least they have a table*, she thought to herself. *At
least they have a Coleman stove and not an old oil
drum*. And at least they had a dream, which was
probably the main difference between the squalor
here and the squalor on Reeker's Hill. Presently
they passed around hot cider in crude hand-
thrown pottery mugs, which proved to have rum
in it. She curled her hands around the mug and
felt the warmth returning.

They talked of art, poetry, and agricultural sci-
ences. Mother Grey felt very comfortable, at least
in spirit. It was a trip back into a less morally
complicated time. She almost didn't want to hear
what she had come all this way to hear.

"So you want to know all about Jerry," said Freed at last, pushing himself away from the table.

She had a sudden flash of memory, Phyllis at the kitchen table with her glass of sherry saying, "You might not like the results." *Maybe not, after all.* But she said, "Yes, tell me whatever you can."

Freed took a hefty drink of cider, a faraway look in his eyes. "When I first knew him, we were students at Rutgers together. He was a crazy guy, he'd do anything for a laugh. Sunshine settled him down a lot."

"His girlfriend."

"Yeah, Sunshine was his woman."

"What was his relationship with his father like?"

"About normal. They hated each other's guts."

She laughed. She thought he was joking, although it was true that many of the hippies were alienated from their families and invested their trust and affection in their friends.

"After I got out of school and started the first Perelandra, Jerry and Sunshine were looking for a place to live, so we let them have the back bedroom. Perelandra wasn't quite a full-blown commune then; it was more like a place where kindred spirits who couldn't afford to rent a place by themselves could move in together and share expenses."

"Tell me about the time you all got arrested."

"Ah. That. Nothing much to tell. The cops came around at three in the morning and busted everybody. Well, not everybody. Sunshine was in Canada trying to find a place for herself and Jerry to live where the draft board wouldn't get him. But the rest of us all got arrested. It was a mighty unpleasant time."

"Then what happened?"

"Eventually everybody made bail. When the case came to trial, we all got probation, except for Marcia. She was dealing and had to do some time." He sighed. "I never see any of those people anymore, the old Perelandrians. One by one they all turned off, tuned out, and dropped in."

"So Jerry forsook the old ideals."

"Jerry was the first."

"Did he ever get to Canada?"

"Father Dad came and collected him from the jailhouse after we got busted. I understand there was a man-to-man talk about the family honor and stuff like that. Next thing we knew he was in the army. I never heard from Sunshine again; I don't know if she had the baby up there or what."

"So Jerry was killed in the war?"

"No, after his discharge he managed to get back here before he hanged himself. He was doing a lot of drugs."

"What a sad story."

"Yeah, well. You win some, you lose some."

"What was her full name?"

"Sunshine?"

"Yes."

"I don't remember. Warner, Walters, something like that."

"Wagonner?"

243

"That was it."

"Phyllis Wagonner."

"That was her name," he said. "But we all called her Sunshine." Something cold and wet touched Mother Grey's face.

It was a flake of snow.

20

She was lying on the ground without her air mattress, something like a rolled blanket supporting her head. She felt cold. Big wet snowflakes drifted out of a charcoal sky and lit on her face like soft insects, like cold kisses. Some strident sound had awakened her, but now it was quiet. Snow falling, hissing.

The blanket didn't smell like her own blanket; it was somebody else's. Something was wrong. *I should get in the tent*, she thought.

The strident sound again, loud static, a human voice buzzing unintelligibly. Police radio. She turned her head toward the sound; there were lights; the snow was glowing. The street was full of fire trucks.

The rectory of St. Bede's was burning.

More radio squawks, other voices, shouts. An explosion of papers burst out of the library window. *It's my sheet music*, she thought. Then more music came out the window, shovelful after shov-

elful fluttering to the muddy ground, to be followed by the books, charred, smoking, torn from
their spines.

How did she get here? Had she, too, been
thrown out of the window? Mother Grey began to
take stock of her body. *First of all, I'm alive. I don't
feel pain anywhere.* Well, maybe her throat and
chest. But only when she breathed in. And maybe
her head. None of her bones felt broken.

She was beginning to remember what had happened. *I was in the fire, and I passed out.* She had
left the commune, driven home . . .

When she let herself in, everyone at the rectory
was asleep. She stepped inside and noticed at once
that her space smelled of strangers, of cigarettes
and beer. The cavernous bare living room, which
she liked without any furniture, truth to tell, still
vibrated seemingly with television programs. But
there was moonlight pouring in through the
curtainless windows, and she thought how fine it
would be one day, imagining wallpaper, one or
two good pieces of furniture instead of the packing
crates, perhaps a piano.

She did not open the door to the kitchen. *I won't
fool with the kitchen tonight*, she thought. Worst
case, everything would be dirty, and Saraleigh
would have burned a track in the oak table with
one of her wretched cigarettes. Mother Grey didn't
want to know about that, not yet, not without a
good night's sleep first.

On the newel post was a jug with flowers in it.
For a moment she thought, *Dave Dogg*, but no, he

wasn't really in love with her, and anyway he thought she was a murderess. Murderer. He would never send flowers to a bad guy. Must have been Rex, trying to get back together with Saraleigh. (The idea of Saraleigh herself buying the flowers was completely unimaginable.) Had Rex been in the house? Who had been here in her house while she was away?

Upstairs in the bathroom, she gave Towser a bowl of water, then splashed her face and made a quick pass at brushing her teeth. Snoring sounds came from the library; Saraleigh must be snoring. Mother Grey was tempted to look in on her but left the door closed on second thought and crept into her own room, there to fall into an exhausted sleep, still in her jeans.

Once again there was barking and scratching.

She pried her eyes open to see Towser making a fuss at the window. Outside on the ledge the massive form of Ralph Voercker was perched somehow, knocking and banging, a bizarre apparition. Mother Grey had never seen him before without his shirt on. He looked strangely white.

Why was he out there in the cold with nothing on but his trousers? Why was he out there at all?

"Mother Vinnie! Get up! The rectory's on fire!"

Smoke was dribbling into the bedroom through the cracks around the door, like a queer gray upside-down waterfall, pooling on the ceiling. The pool was coming down, pressing closer. As she got out of bed, her feet found the bunny slippers and she took hold of the dog and a woolen blanket.

Woolen blankets are good in a fire. They don't flame up. Crouching low, she got to the window and pushed it open.

"We gotta get out of here," said Ralph. He helped her and the dog out onto the ledge. He was very strong. He held the dog under one arm. There was enough tread on the bunny slippers for Mother Grey to keep her footing.

"Are we supposed to leave the window open or closed?" she said. "I can't remember." Closed, maybe; open was for a tornado.

"Let's just go," said Ralph, edging toward the porch roof. The concrete paving was maybe eighteen feet below, too far to jump. "Saraleigh and the kids are on the porch roof. I need to help them get down." Following after Ralph, she worked her way around the narrow ledge until she could stand almost comfortably on the roof of the porch.

Indeed, the Kanes were there waiting in night-clothes and blankets to go through it all again. Poor things.

"You go first, Saraleigh, and then we'll lower the kids down to you," Ralph said. He took Saraleigh by her plump wrists and slowly let her down to the point where she could grab the drainpipe and get her feet on the porch rail. When Saraleigh was safely down, Mother Grey and Ralph made a sling out of the blanket and lowered the baby to her. Then they used it to let Towser down.

"You hand Freddy down to me, Mother Vinnie," said Ralph. He climbed slowly down, a tremendous strain on the drainpipe. "After we get Freddy down, you come down, Mother. Right, Fred? We'll make sure Mother's feet go in the right place. If you slip, I'll be there to catch you, Mother Vinnie." She had never seen him so manly and competent. But whatever was he doing here? If not for the bite of the wind, she would have thought it a dream.

Light from the fire, coming through the un-curtained windows, flickered on Saraleigh's face in the yard below. "It's really goin'," she said. "Good thing you ain't got nothin' valuable in there."

"Oh, my soul," said Mother Grey. "The Weaver." Priceless artifact, sweet singer, the very last thing she owned that had been Mother's.

"You mean the cello?" said Freddy. "I know where it is. I can get it for you easy."

"Oh, Freddy, *no!*" But it was too late; before she could stop him, he was back inside the library win-dow. For a second she stood paralyzed, not quite believing that he'd gone back in there, and for her. Then, naturally, she went in after him.

It was very hard to see, but not as bad as what she was expecting; there was a good four feet of clear air near the floor. "Fred! Come out! Forget the cello, it isn't that important!"

"It's all right, Mother Grey," the boy called from low down somewhere in the darkness. "I've got it. It's right over here. I played on it while you were gone. Pretty lucky, huh?"

"Get out, Fred, before you get hurt. Keep your head down, and come this way." It was getting hotter. She heard him coughing. "Come on. Honey, come with me."

"Mother Grey?" he said, very faint and far away.

Keep down. "Put your head down by the floor," she called. "Keep talking to me. I'll find you." She could hear the fire hissing.

"It's hot," he said. More coughing, and then no sound at all.

If only she had a flashlight. She groped her way along the wall, then whacked her forehead on something hard, like an iron pipe, and realized it was the fold-out couch. Well, then, the door must be over this way. Working her way around the couch, she put out her hand and touched the cool, buttery surface of the Weaver, lying on its side out of its case. "Fred?" she said. But the boy didn't answer.

Everyone outside was yelling for them to come out. Ralph seemed to be trying to get back on the porch roof and failing. She heard a loud sound of the drainpipe ripping, Ralph falling, cursing, and then all of them yelling. Then the sounds grew fainter and the smoke grew thicker, and she thought maybe it was just a dream after all.

So how had she gotten here on the sidewalk? And what had become of Fred?

There was a plastic thing over her nose and mouth, hissing. She realized that she wasn't lying entirely on the sidewalk; actually, someone was holding her. She pulled off the oxygen mask and got a big whiff of smoke and manly armpit.

"Hey, Vinnie. Vinnie." So Dave Dogg was back.

His lips were against her ear. *If I weren't feeling so ill*, she thought, *this could be quite pleasant.* Firefighters with leather hats and black nostrils came and bent over her. "She's coming out of it," one of them said.

"Is Freddy all right?" she tried to ask them, but a fit of coughing seized her and she was unable to get the words out. "Take it easy," Dave Dogg said.

She tried again to speak. "Be sick" was all she could say, and then she was. He held her head. He gave her some tissues. *I could love this man with very little effort.*

After a moment's rest she managed to ask, "Freddy?"

"Freddy's gonna make it," said Dave Dogg. "We got him out in time. He's in the ambulance, on his way to the medical center. When I found you, you had hold of his ankle, luckily."

She didn't remember finding Freddy. So Dave Dogg had saved her life. And Freddy's. But why was there a fire? Cigarettes? Wiring? The furnace? The television. She knew there was some good reason not to have a television in the house. There were statistics someplace on the number of fires started by television sets every year; it was phenomenal; Grandmother had unplugged hers whenever she wasn't using it.

"Torch job," said a voice nearby.

"Yeah?" said Dave Dogg.

"Stinks of kerosene all over the first floor. Somebody burned her out on purpose."

A blast of dog breath, and there was Towser, licking her face. Ralph, still half-naked, was with the dog; he crouched down to talk to her where she lay.

"Your shirt," she said to him. Talking hurt; otherwise, she would have had a great deal more to say.

"I left it in Saraleigh's bedroom," he said. "Mother, I gotta tell you something before you hear it someplace else. Saraleigh and me, well, she's my girlfriend."

"My word."

"I know this is kind of sudden."

She tried to sit up. Now what was Ralph getting himself into? "Ralph, does this mean . . ."

"We're going to look for a place to live," he said. "I guess you don't know of anything."

A place to live. She slumped back down again and found herself in Dave Dogg's lap. Towser was all black again. He would have to have another bath, but in what bathtub? Smoke and flames were roiling out of the rectory's bathroom window. "We're all homeless now," she said. What a life.

"Oh, shit, that's right. I hadn't thought of that. It's a problem. But we'll work something out."

"Ralph," she said feebly. He started and looked guilty. "Take care of Towser."

"Okay, Mother Grey. Okay. Don't worry about a thing," as his face grew longer and longer.

She realized he thought she was dying, right there in the arms of Dave Dogg, but that was not at all what she was trying to convey; actually she was feeling better by the minute, although it was very, very hard to talk. She tried again. "I'm okay," she said. "I can't talk. Just take him."

"Towser?" said Ralph.

"To the vet," she said. Why was he making her talk? It hurt.

"Oh. Okay," he said. He picked the dog up in his arms and carried him away in the direction of the veterinarian's office, glancing back anxiously every so often. She watched him until he was out of sight. Sheila would board the dog for her, and with luck she would have sense enough to make Ralph put a shirt on. It was too cold to run around without a shirt. She shivered. Dave Dogg held her a little tighter.

He had saved her life. Now he was wrapping her in his jacket. And all the time he thought she was a murderer. There was something important she had to tell him. "It was Phyllis," she said.

"Forget about it," said Dave Dogg. "Don't worry. The other ambulance will get here in a minute." He had no idea what she was trying to tell him. "Get some rest." Another blackened face appeared.

"How ya doing, Mother Vinnie?" It was Jack Kreevitch.

She had a coughing fit, and then she answered, "Fine."

"You want the oxygen mask again?" said Dave Dogg.

"No. Phyllis—"

"I think Brother Rex must have torched the rectory," said Kreevitch. "Somebody did, anyways. There's accelerant in there from hell to breakfast. Kerosene, looks like."

"What would he do that for?" said Dave Dogg.

"Our friend Ralph was shacked up in there with Rex's woman," said Kreevitch. "Probably he was jealous. Hate to tell you this, Mother Vinnie, but Saraleigh has been raising hell while you were gone."

The whole town knew. Good heavens, what would Mrs. van Buskirk say?

"So what's your plan?" said Dave Dogg.

"Goin' up the hill to Hotel Ford and arrest him. He's a mean son of a bitch, probably armed, but this has gone far enough."

"Let me come with you," said Dave Dogg. "Just wait till the ambulance gets here for Vinnie."

"I don't want to hang around any longer than I have to," said Kreevitch. "He might sober up and start running."

"Phyllis," she said again.

"Here comes Phyllis," said Kreevitch.

"Here's Phyllis, Vinnie," Dave Dogg said. "We'll get her to take care of you till the ambulance comes. It shouldn't be more than a minute." He kissed her forehead.

She tried, with a grip surprisingly weak, to take him by the sleeve. "Don't! Not Phyllis—" but he put her gently down, pillowing her head on the blanket.

She saw him talking to Phyllis, gesturing, the two of them silhouetted against the lights and smoke, and then he followed Kreevitch. The two policemen threaded their way between parked fire trucks and were gone. *I'd better see if I can get up.* It was harder than she expected, but she made it to her feet. And there stood Phyllis.

"Hello, Vinnie," she said.

"Hello, Sunshine," said Mother Grey.

"I've come to take you home."

"I have no home," said Mother Grey, and as she spoke the porch roof of the rectory collapsed with a terrible crash.

"I'm taking you to my home." Phyllis put an arm around her shoulder, holding her firmly. Mother Grey didn't remember her being so strong. There was a smell of kerosene on Phyllis's hands; kerosene. Accelerant. It was Phyllis who had burned her house down. She tried to shake her off, to push her away, to cry out to the firemen, to anybody, but her voice failed, her strength failed, as Phyllis bore her relentlessly toward the car.

Across an ocean of wet street where reflected flames glistened in the water, the firemen, working fiercely, kept their faces turned toward the burning house. She tried to shout, "Help me!" But it was like one of those nightmares where nothing comes out but a whisper.

She was in the car, still struggling. Something malodorous and sickly sweet was pressing on her nose and mouth. Then the car spun around and around and fell into a bottomless hole.

* * *

"Hope you got cleats in these tires," Dave Dogg said. The snow was turning into a nasty freezing rain.

"Don't need cleats," said Jack Kreevitch. "My driving skills carry me through." He jammed on the brakes, throwing Fishersville Police Cruiser number three into a spin that put them onto Reeker's Hill Road, facing the right way somehow. "Power slide," said Kreevitch. From there Dave Dogg could see that the road went almost straight up.

"Maybe we should wait for the city to salt the road," Dave Dogg suggested. "I mean, how far can Rex Perskie get in this kind of weather?"

"City doesn't salt this road. No point in it. Nobody ever comes up here. Hold on."

Kreevitch backed up a little and, getting a running start, began to fishtail up the hill with such a whining and screaming of back tires that Brother Rex could surely hear them coming a mile away. Suddenly the car hit a bad patch and plunged nose first into the ditch.

"Help me pull it out," said Kreevitch, hopping out of the car.

Slowly Dave Dogg got out his side. Was this enterprise worth a hernia? "How much farther is it?" he said.

"Quarter of a mile."

"Tell you what," said Dogg. "Let's walk. Then when we get back, we can make Brother Rex pull it out."

"I don't think that's legal," said Kreevitch. "But okay."

Dave Dogg's feet were freezing by the time they got to the homeless camp. A crust of ice was forming on top of two inches of soft snow, and it broke noisily whenever they stepped on it. Whatever campers there were must have heard them coming, *crunch, crunch,* but as they came into the clearing with the flaming oil drum, no one was in sight.

The people were inside the cars.

Blankets and tarpaulins were arranged over the broken windows and missing doors of the disabled vehicles, and the ice had crusted on these too. Jack Kreevitch knocked on the roof of one of the cars, and a muffled voice came from inside.

"I'm looking for Rex Perskie," said Kreevitch. "Seen him?"

Meanwhile Dave Dogg eyeballed the snow all around the clearing and beyond for signs of fleeing footprints. There were none. No one had left the cars since the ice began to cake on top of the snow.

One by one Jack Kreevitch went around to all the cars and vans while Dave Dogg kept a lookout. With some of them he had to break the ice on the blankets that were keeping the wind and rain out so he could see whether Rex was inside. But he wasn't. Everyone who knew Rex told him the same thing: Rex hadn't been there in three days.

"How can they stand it, living like that?" Dave Dogg said as they crunched back down the hill.

"You drink enough, you can stand anything," said Kreevitch.

"Maybe so," said Dave Dogg. The police cruiser was stuck well and truly. It did not respond to pulling, pushing, rocking, cramming things under the wheel for traction, or any of the usual remedies for a stuck car. So Jack radioed back to the police station for a tow truck.

"Chief Harry wants to know what you're doing up there," the dispatcher said.

"Looking for Rex Perskie."

"Why?"

"He burned down Mother Grey's rectory, is why. Ain't you heard the sirens?"

"Chief Harry says Rex is in Florida."

"What the hell's he doing in Florida?"

"He's in the slammer in Tallahassee. Got himself picked up for assault and battery two days ago. A bar fight or something like that. Police called up to find out if we wanted him for anything in Fishersville. Chief Harry said, no, we sure didn't."

Jack Kreevitch thanked the dispatcher and settled in to wait for the tow truck. "So who torched the rectory?" Dave Dogg said.

"Beats me," said Kreevitch. "Maybe some other friend of Saraleigh's."

Dave Dogg rubbed his hands together. Feeling was returning to them, and the feeling was pain. He took his shoes off and massaged his wet feet. "I can't sit here," he said. "I need to get back to someplace warm."

"I'll turn up the heater," said Kreevitch. He revved the engine.

"Why don't we walk back to town?" said Dave Dogg. "It can't be that far." Something was wrong, he could feel it. If it wasn't Rex who had set that fire. . . .

"If I leave this car up here," said Kreevitch, "I'll come back and find the hubcaps gone and a family of five living in it. Sit tight. There's plenty of time."

21

Mother Grey's head hurt. It was hard to breathe for some reason. She felt sick again, but she was able to slip away from the feeling by going back to sleep. While she slept, she had a dream: She was five years old, and her parents were taking her to visit Hyde Park.

Far below the road where they were driving, the Hudson River spread out before them, sparkling in the sunlight, full of gray ships. "That's the mothball fleet, Vinnie," her father said. Sure enough, she noticed a smell of mothballs. Then the pain came back and after that the nausea, and she was awake, lying on the floor of a smelly closet.

Before her eyes was a shoebag full of faintly familiar nine-and-a-halfs, neatly paired. *Gunboats*, she thought. They must be Phyllis's. Who else would be neurotic enough to keep a night light burning in the closet?

I'd better get out of here. She tried to move, but there was something holding her; she tried to shout, but there was something over her mouth. Tape. She had tape all over her.

Again she felt that she might vomit, but she fought the urge, fearing to choke to death. *I've got to get out.* There was no real doorknob on the inside of the closet, just a tiny little knob like one you might use to open a lock. Mother Grey couldn't find a way to get a purchase on it.

Gunboats. How was it that she had never noticed the huge size of Phyllis's feet before? To see her entire shoe collection together in one place was a truly awe-inspiring experience, almost like visiting Sequoia National Park. Then she heard them coming, those clunky great pedal extremities, on the stairs, on the rug, outside the closet door.

The latch clicked; the door swung open. There she stood. *The fleet's in.*

"Vinnie, I'm *so* sorry I had to tie you up like this," said Phyllis, "and tape your mouth, and all that good stuff, but we both know about your legendary powers of persuasion, and I just don't want to *hear* it. I have to do what I have to do."

She carried a big bucket of water in one hand. What was it that she felt she had to do?

"Oh, well," she said. She put the bucket down. "I might as well let you be comfortable for a while." She picked Mother Grey up in her arms and dropped her on the bed, among the stuffed bears, like a rag doll. "I want to tell you what this is all about first," she said. "I owe you an explanation."

"You owe me to get this tape off my mouth," Mother Grey tried to say, but all that came out was a loud, indignant humming.

Phyllis yanked her by the hair and said, "Stop that before I tape your nose too. I want you to just listen to me."

I always listen to you. Then she had to really listen to her, if only to take her mind off the idea of what it would be like to have Phyllis tape her nose, and not ever be able to get her breath again.

"With your poking around, which you will recall I warned you against, I suppose you found out about me and Jerry Wealle," Phyllis said. "Did they tell you the bishop broke us up? We were going to go to Canada and get married and have the baby and everything. I was all set to meet him up there, but his dad talked him out of it and he went off to war instead. But I already told you that part of the story; let me get to the good stuff." How do you tell if a person is crazy? It's in the eyes. Phyllis was crazy. There was white showing all around the irises, a demented stare, terrifying. Mother Grey found that meeting her gaze intensified her claustrophobic panic. She looked at different places around the room and tried to think of other things while Phyllis explained just how it was that she had come to murder the Bishop of New Jersey.

"I figured he was going to be at this convention, but I didn't think I was going to have to see him to speak to. There wasn't any reason why he should recognize me. I had only met him once, one

Christmas, when Jerry took me home with him. I've changed a lot since then.

"But I went downstairs to the lower lobby, and there he was. I was only going to give him the pamphlet and say something nice about St. Bede's, but something made me identify myself to him. 'I'm Phyllis Wagonner, Bishop Wealle,' I said.

"He said, 'Phyllis. Of course. How are you, my dear?' and then he stood looking off in space for a long time.

"Then he said—get this—'I've often wished that you and Jerry had been married.' He wished that, he said. As if he hadn't been the one who broke us up. I wanted him to look at me and say it. He wasn't even looking at me. He bent over that drinking fountain. He was having a drink. I wanted him to look me in the face and say it again.

"So I reached out and took hold of the chain he wore around his neck—I was just going to make him look at me—

"Something happened to his neck. It was almost completely by accident.

"And yet.

"I couldn't bring myself to feel sorry, Vinnie. In fact . . . in fact . . . suddenly I realized that I felt wonderful, exhilarated, empowered. All those years of hating this man, resenting him, fearing him, and now with my own two hands I had personally sent him to Hell, where he belonged. Well, of course I knew there would be trouble over it. So I put him in the cloakroom. It was easy enough. He wasn't difficult to move; even though he was so tall, he hardly weighed anything. The floor was smooth. I just took one arm and one leg and dragged him out of sight and let the door close on him. That was that.

"It never crossed my mind that anyone would suspect Ralph. Or you, of all people. The idea of your killing the bishop." She laughed. "But killing people, Vinnie . . . you ought to try it. The feeling it gives you, I can't tell you what a thrill it is. I haven't been depressed for a single minute since I murdered the bishop. If I start to feel low, all I have to do is think of him lying there at my mercy to get high all over again.

"Well, okay, not really at my mercy. After all, he was dead and quite beyond that. *You're* at my mercy. And that's too bad for you, Vinnie, because I really don't have any mercy. Mercy is not where it's at with me." She looked at the pail, and then back at Vinnie, lying taped and helpless on the bed, and then she took a deep breath, let it sharply out through her mouth, and continued with her story.

"I suppose you're wondering about that boy," she said. "He tried to blackmail me. Can you imagine? After he left that note in my mailbox—the one I planted on your desk for dear Dave to find—I called him and arranged for a meeting at the wing dam early the next morning. He came roaring up on one of those detestable motorized dirt bikes, disturbing the waterfowl and the country all around, making a horrible racket. If you weren't so deep into all this God stuff, Vinnie, I'm sure you would agree that anyone who rides one of those things in a state park deserves death.

"I told him we should go out onto the dam so that nobody would overhear us. Since he had seen me kill the bishop, he didn't think I was very dangerous—I told you it was an accident, I was innocent, almost—and he had no fear of coming out there with me. Probably he didn't realize about the current or the rocks. He wasn't expecting it. I just pushed him in. He hit his head and drowned right away, sank from sight, it was as though he had never been. The dirt bike went in after him, washed under the dam by the rip.

"And that was that. But then I realized I was going to have to put the blame on someone. So I planted the blackmail note on your desk. I'm sorry about that.

"No, I'm not sorry, actually. You know, Vinnie, I really hate you. You are so happy, in this weird fool's paradise. Everyone loves you. Strange men come to town and fall for you. It isn't fair. If I didn't do anything about it, you would marry Dave Dogg, and in four or five years you'd have three little red-headed babies."

I hate you, too, Phyllis, thought Mother Grey, and gazed at the open closet door, where the mothball fleet lay at anchor. *I hate you 'cause your feet's too big. I hate you because you never shut up. I hate you because maybe I'd like to have red-headed babies with Dave Dogg, and instead of that I'm going to die here.* She had figured out what it was that Phyllis meant to do with the pail of water.

She was going to take Mother Grey, all taped up and helpless as she was, and stick her head in the pail until she drowned.

"Here's your suicide note," Phyllis said proudly, following Mother Grey's train of thought. "I think the signature is rather good, don't you? It says you're sorry for what you did, and rather than face the shame of a trial, you're going to throw yourself in the river. My plan, as if you didn't know, is to leave this where your good friend Dave will find it. Then I can take your body to the river and throw it in whenever I feel like it, and when they fish it out, the case will be closed. Of course, I have to drown you first.

"But before I do that, I think I'll preach you a sermon for a change. You with your pitiful efforts in that dilapidated church, trying to carry on with one old lady and a feeb. What do you think you're accomplishing? Those precious alcoholics of yours —you know they're going right back to the bottle, don't you? Your battered women—you know they're going right home to get beat up again. And why should you care? Nobody cares. God himself doesn't care.

"Do you think He cares? The Lord of the Bosnians, the Lord of the Somalis? The Lord of the Jews, for Christ's sake. Babies in the ovens. You probably think he's going to intervene right now and save you from me, don't you? I'd like to know what you think you did to deserve His particular attention.

"Curse God and die, Vinnie. You're doomed,

and if anyone cares, it isn't God. We might as well get started." Thus ended the homily. Phyllis reached over to grab Mother Grey and pick her up.

But Mother Grey was prepared to be uncooperative. She drew up her knees and lashed out with her bound feet, striking Phyllis squarely in the solar plexus.

Winded, Phyllis stood holding herself. Mother Grey rolled off the bed and toward the door. Before she could reach it, Phyllis got her arm and tried for a hammerlock, but with her wrists bound together the arm wouldn't bend that way. Mother Grey wriggled out of her grip and tried again to get to the stairs.

Then the pail went over, flooding the room, staining the rug, and thoroughly enraging Phyllis. "That was river water!" she cried, and grabbed Mother Grey by the head in a grip she could not shake off. "You miserable bitch!" She pinched Mother Grey's nostrils together, shutting off her last gasping breath. "I carried that all the way from the river so the autopsy would look right! Now look at this mess, just look at it. The plaster will probably come down in Mother's room. I could kill you." This was the last thing Mother Grey heard as light and sound faded, this and a ringing noise that resolved itself into a knocking.

Then suddenly her head was on the floor, and she was breathing. Phyllis had let her drop. "I'll take care of you later," she said. "Someone is at the door. Make all the noise you want, nobody can hear you up here.''

She breathed in great lungfuls of air, as much as she could with her mouth taped, until the light came back completely and her mind cleared. *I have to get out.* She worked her tongue, trying to dislodge the tape, but it was too big and there was too much of it. Her fingers were free, although her hands were taped behind her; she struggled to her feet and then slipped and fell on the wet rug. She got up again, hopped clumsily to the door, tried the knob. Locked.

She threw her weight against it with a loud thumping noise that surely could be heard by whoever was visiting. The door stood fast. No one came. Supporting herself against the wall, she made her way to the window and found that it was unlocked.

By getting her shoulder under the sash and using the strength of her knees to push it upward, Mother Grey was able to open the window all the way. It had no screen on it. Evidently she was in the tower room, many feet from the driveway below, much too far to jump or fall without risking almost certain death. For a moment, Mother Grey considered jumping anyway; almost anything would be better than having Phyllis come back and hold her nose again. There was a police car parked in the drive, lights flashing.

Maybe Jack Kreevitch and Dave had come to save her. She hung out of the window as far as she dared. Yes, it was them, Jack in his uniform hat and Dave Dogg, bareheaded, with a little bald spot starting in the back. Probably he had freckles there too. She could see Phyllis's hands sticking out of the front door, gesturing. One of the hands held a white envelope. Dave Dogg reached out, took it, and opened it to reveal a piece of yellow paper; it was the so-called suicide note that Phyllis had been waving around a few moments before.

If only she could call out to him or signal him somehow. She rattled the sash, but the sound was insignificant and didn't carry. *I'll drop something down on them.* One of her slippers. She knelt down and got her bunny slipper off somehow and then backed up to the window and threw it out, as hard as she could manage to with her wrists taped. But her cast lacked sufficient force. The slipper caught in the second-floor gutter and stared up at her, pink and reproachful.

By this time, both Dogg and Kreevitch had read the note through and were evidently completely taken in by it. They stared at the note, and then at each other, and then they ran for the waiting police car. With a scream of tires and sirens they were gone.

The front door slammed shut; Mother Grey heard the knocker bounce once. *She's coming.* There was a ledge of roof outside the tower window, but it was steeply pitched and only about a foot wide. Even if Mother Grey had been in her full strength and not bound or gagged, she would have hesitated to venture out there. As it was, she wouldn't consider it. But Phyllis didn't know that, did she? Phyllis thought Mother Grey could walk on water.

Phyllis's clumping footsteps were on the stairs, getting closer. Mother Grey's telltale bunny slipper was clearly visible in the gutter outside the window. *Evidence of my escape.* As the lock of the door began to rattle, before the door itself could swing open, Mother Grey rolled under the bed and lay among the dust mice, not making a sound.

To all appearances the room Phyllis Wagonner burst into was quite empty. Twin gunboats steamed toward the open window. "Vinnie?" Phyllis called, and then she muttered, "Shit." Mother Grey could hear her getting a leg up onto the windowsill, the better to see whether she might be hiding on the roof.

Then there was a scrabbling noise as of tearing shingles, and a screech—"Wow!"—and then a sound like that of someone dropping a large watermelon a long way.

Even with all that, Mother Grey waited several minutes before she came out from under the bed. It could be a ruse. Phyllis might be tricking her, waiting to pinch her nostrils shut again as soon as she showed her nose.

Quietly Mother Grey knelt in front of the window and slowly, slowly put out her head. She half expected to feel iron fingers closing on her. But Phyllis wasn't waiting on the roof. Then she looked down, and for an instant she thought to see enormous feet protruding from under the house, clad in a pair of immense ruby slippers. But Phyllis wasn't under the house, either; rather, she was beside it, lying motionless, staring up at Mother Grey, apparently perfectly conscious.

"Vinnie," she called.

Mother Grey grunted and nodded.

"Vinnie, help me. I think my neck is broken."

Mother Grey nodded again. *I'll get an ambulance.*

And she did, by a series of undignified activities that involved propelling herself around the house on her bottom in search of a telephone and then scraping the tape off her face on a doorjamb so that she could speak to call for help. It took a long time to make her way outside. The Fishersville rescue squad siren had begun to wail by the time Mother Grey reached the front steps.

Phyllis lay sprawled on her back, motionless, her limbs at unnatural angles, her chest rising and falling in quick shallow breaths. "The ambulance is on its way," Mother Grey said. "Are you in much pain?"

"I can't feel anything. Vinnie, I'm frightened. Pray for me."

Mother Grey, her ankles still bound, her hands still taped together behind her back, gazed at her former friend the way she would have looked at a half-dead snake. Phyllis had murdered two innocent people, one of them young; she had tried to incinerate Mother Grey and had succeeded in destroying almost all of her meager material possessions; she had nearly smothered her; she had tried to drown her. "One thing I don't understand. Why the baby? I can see that you wanted to burn me to death to keep me from turning you in, but how could you set fire to a house with a sleeping baby in it? I thought you loved babies.''

"Why should Saraleigh have that baby?" Phyllis replied.

Mother Grey nearly said, "Pray for your own self, Phyllis.'' The words were almost out of her mouth. Mother Grey had never experienced such hostility for another human being in her entire life. Fortunately the priest in her overcame the woman, and she said to Phyllis, "I will pray for you.'' Fortunately, because in the next moment Phyllis Wagonner took one long rasping breath and then stopped breathing altogether.

22

Mother Grey sat down on the steps of Phyllis Wagonner's front porch and leaned her head against one of the pillars. It was curious how the paint, which looked so white and flawless at a distance, was checked with tiny dirt-filled cracks if you put your face right up to it. The pillar felt cool against her head, though; she closed her eyes. Presently she realized that she was crying. Now that Phyllis was gone, the work of crying had to be carried on by somebody else.

How could I not have known? I was her therapist. If only I had done my job in a halfway competent manner, I could have saved the lives of three people. Yet it was said that psychopaths were very devious and clever and could fool anybody. Was that what Phyllis was, a psychopath? As far as Mother Grey was aware, she had never known a psychopath; she had no standard against which to measure her.

When Dave Dogg arrived with the ambulance,

she was still crying, her slow tears running in a little track down the side of the painted white pillar. He wasn't with the ambulance, exactly, but they seemed to drive up at the same time. While the ambulance crew worked with Phyllis, Dave Dogg took Mother Grey in his arms and comforted her, wiping her tears away like those of a little child.

"I'm sorry," she said. She felt very foolish. It had been years since anyone else had wiped her nose.

"No," he said, "I'm sorry. I don't know how I could have thought—" He peeled all the tape off her. "Let's get you out of this."

Then he kissed her, she couldn't tell whether from relief that she was safe, or passion, or just to congratulate her for escaping death and triumphing over evil. She found herself kissing him back.

"She's gone," said one of the ambulance attendants. "There's nothing we can do for her." He looked up at the tower and down at Mother Grey and the pile of tape. "How did—?"

"Jack Kreevitch will take her statement," said Dave Dogg. "Mother Grey can't talk right now. I'll drive her to the emergency room at County Medical Center. You guys take care of . . . that." He gestured toward Phyllis.

So she got in his car and they drove away, leaving Phyllis's empty house with its comforts and riches far behind them. Landmarks drifted past them, the burned house, the road to Reeker's Hill, the highway shopping center where the county housing agency had its offices. The sun was out. The snow was melting away.

"Want to talk?" he said.

She said, "No. No, thank you." She wanted to be quiet, to invite some sort of peace. In the emergency room she let him hold her hand while she waited for her turn to see the doctors. There were people ahead of her, mothers with sick or injured children, a young man having a bad drug experience. The young man's girlfriend or wife was with him. She thought of the night she had first come here with Ralph.

A nurse came and ushered them into the emergency treatment room, where Mother Grey was made to lie on a gurney behind some curtains. A doctor looked at her bruises and listened to her chest. A technician brought a black machine with a dial on top and a hole in the end and made her put her finger in it. "To see whether your blood needs oxygen," she said, with what was evidently meant to be a reassuring smile. Apparently the results were satisfactory, for they gave her no oxygen, neither did they stick her with needles. Yet they did not encourage her to leave the hospital.

"We would like to keep you overnight for observation," the doctor said. Dave Dogg trailed along while they wheeled her to another part of the hospital and found her a room. Indeed, he stayed until the health care professionals chased him away.

"I'll come get you tomorrow," he said.

There were two beds in her room, but the other one was empty. Once she was tucked in and everyone had gone away, she felt terrible. She started to cry again.

This is stupid, she thought. At least she could blow her own nose. *Tomorrow I'll get up out of this bed and go save St. Bede's.* There was much to be done. The archdeacon was coming any day now. How long had she been in Phyllis's closet? What day was it?

"They told me you were in here," came a voice from the doorway. There stood Saraleigh, wearing a whole new getup. The outfit was so like the other one that Ralph must have picked it out. "Are you okay?" said Saraleigh. "Where ya been?"

"At Phyllis Wagonner's house," said Mother Grey. It was amazing the things people donated to church thrift shops. Who would buy high-heeled white patent leather lace-up ankle boots in the first place? Or, having realized how foolish it was to buy them, who would think anyone at a church thrift shop would want them?

"Phyllis took care of you, did she?" Saraleigh was chewing gum. Her hair looked more than usually rumpled.

Took care of me? "Very nearly."

"The baby and me were up all night sittin' in a chair in Fred's room."

"Poor Freddy. How is he?"

"Good. They might let him come home tomorrow."

Thank God. "But where's home going to be, Saraleigh?"

"I don't know yet. Your friend Father Spelving

told some people about us, and they said maybe we could stay at this church in town, for a week anyways."

"He put you in touch with the Interfaith Hospitality Network."

"Yeah."

"Have you been back to St. Bede's?"

"Not today. While you were away, some guys came around measuring the windows."

"The windows!"

"Yeah. Some priest, and he had like a workman with him. They came in a truck. You having anything done to the windows?"

"No. They could use a little work, but we can't afford it." *Who in the world?* "What did the priest look like?"

"Heavy-set guy. Bald head."

Bingley! "He's not heavy-set, he's fat. So he was measuring my windows, was he! Where are my clothes?"

"Hey, take it easy. You're supposed to lie down and rest."

"I want my clothes. I have to get out of here." Her things seemed to be gone, and all she had to put on her feet was one bunny slipper. "Could you go and ask them what happened to—"

"Dave took your clothes," said Saraleigh.

"Dave Dogg took my clothes."

"I seen him going out. I guess he was going to wash them or something. You wouldn't want to wear 'em the way they was."

"No, I suppose not." She felt her face. It was a

little hot. Maybe she should rest now. "Did you get hold of anybody on the vestry?"

"You were right about the vestry," Saraleigh said, cracking her gum. "They're mostly dead. The others were wondering what was up, but I couldn't tell 'em. What is up? Do you want me to tell 'em?"

"Saraleigh, what day is it?"

"Saturday, why?"

"Oh, this is awful. The Archdemon is coming tomorrow to close my church."

"How can he do that?"

"Nobody ever comes to church, and last year I had to bury half the vestry." She held her head in her hands. "And now Father Bingley wants my windows."

"Well, he ain't gonna get 'em." Saraleigh put her hands on her hips. "Jesus, if I knew what he was up to, I would have fixed his fat rear, him and that guy he had with him. I know how to treat people like them. You just leave everything to me and Ralphie, Mother Vinnie." She turned and started out the door, heels clacking.

"What are you going to do?"

From halfway down the hall came her voice: "Trust me."

23

"I brought you some clothes." Dave Dogg came in with her things almost before she had finished the hospital's idea of breakfast. "Here's your jacket too. Since we know who killed the bishop, it isn't evidence. They said at the nurses' station you could go home. What were you doing in the middle of the night last night?"

"I don't know. I guess I got up." So it wasn't a dream. They had found her roaming the halls of the medical center clad only in two hospital gowns (one turned back-to-front for decency's sake) and the bunny slipper. She remembered feeling that she had to save St. Bede's. The Lord would surely show her the way to some size-six outer garments, whereupon she could get into them and go home. How she was to get back to Fishersville, she couldn't have said. "Maybe I was sleepwalking. It felt like a dream."

How embarrassing. At least no one was telling her this morning that she was too crazy to leave.

"The skirt that matches my jacket is burned up," Mother Grey said.

"Win some, lose some. Wear it with the jeans. It'll look great."

"What am I going to do for shoes?"

He reached in his coat pocket and took out a pair of black Chinese slippers.

"Don't tell me. You just happened to have these in your closet."

"Got 'em at the Jamesway," he said.

"Thank you." She wasn't sure she would have had the courage to celebrate Mass in one bunny slipper. The Chinese Mary Janes were just the right size. "I wouldn't have thought you noticed the size of my feet."

"I notice your feet. I notice you all over. I want to suck your toes."

"My word."

"Sorry, I didn't mean to be offensive."

"People don't usually say things like that to me."

"I'll stop if you want me to."

"Why don't you just wait downstairs while I get dressed? I'll see you in the lobby."

"I'll just wait downstairs." He left, smiling. She didn't really mind if he said lewd things to her, and he knew it, and she found it disconcerting. But it was not time to wrestle with this now. It was time to prepare to face the empty church and the malevolence of the Archdemon.

She dressed. The ensemble looked great. There would be an extra clerical collar waiting for her in the working sacristy of the church, so she would soon look like her normal self again.

As she was tucking her shirt in, she heard a commotion in the hall. She looked out to see, and here came Freddy Kane in a wheelchair, propelling himself down the corridor at top speed and making *vroom, vroom* noises.

When he saw her, he veered wildly toward her room and ran into the doorjamb.

"Where's the brakes on this thing?" he muttered.

"Well, Freddy," said Mother Grey. "I'm glad to see you up and around. How do you feel?"

"Good, thanks," he said. "Are you going to finish your milk?" Sure enough, she had left half her milk in the glass.

"No, you can have it, Freddy." He drank it, ate the toast, and went running off without his wheelchair. It was too big for him, anyway; he had probably borrowed it from some helpless patient in another ward. *The boy needs to develop a disciplined attitude*, she thought. She would find another cello and give him lessons. It would make a man of him.

The nurses wanted her to ride downstairs in a wheelchair. "If I needed a wheelchair," she said, "I wouldn't leave." She stopped at the business office and took care of the necessary arrangements. The bill was to be sent to St. Bede's. *Surely I'll still be there on Monday when the hospital bookkeeping office opens*.

Dave Dogg was waiting in the lobby. His car was right outside. "Where to, lady?" he said.

"St. Bede's," she said. "Church is in half an hour." With Phyllis dead, the congregation would be down to two. "It might be the last time I'll ever hold services at St. Bede's."

"What, are they going to throw you out because your house burned down?"

"No, it's more complicated than that. But having no rectory doesn't help."

"Where will you go?"

"I still have my camping equipment in the car. I think what I'll do tonight, Dave, is take it up Reeker's Hill Road and camp out at the Hotel Ford."

"Don't do that, Vinnie," he said. "You can't do that. You don't know what it's like up there. What do you think, it's a Scout camp? Those guys are drunks, losers, half of them in trouble with the law. They won't respect your holy orders. Stay at my place."

"Oh, I see. You'll respect my holy orders."

"At least check into a motel."

"I'll be all right. This is something I've been thinking of doing anyway. It's an important ministry."

"I don't suppose you'd like some company up there in your tent," he said.

"No. No, thanks." She was going to have a hard enough time about this with Mrs. van Buskirk. "I'll take Towser. We'll be fine."

Then suddenly he pulled off the highway, swerving into the entrance to the parking lot of the very shopping center where the Housing Authority had its offices. Everything there was closed. The lot was empty. He turned the engine off.

"Vinnie," he began.

"Now, Dave, don't be difficult. I can take care of myself perfectly well. You don't need to worry."

"That's not what I'm trying to say."

"Well, what, then?"

"I want you to marry me."

"My word."

"Stop saying 'my word.' I'm in love with you. I've never met anyone like you. I think we'd be good together. I want to have you around for the rest of my life."

This was distressing. She ran her hands through her hair, feeling the warmth of her own scalp, trying to get in touch with reality.

"You don't have to give me an answer right now." He started the engine again. "I just wanted you to know where I'm coming from." He put the car in gear and rolled toward the highway.

"No, wait," she said. "Wait. We need to finish this conversation." He coasted to a stop and turned the engine off again.

She looked into his eyes. Blue as ever, they were no longer alarmingly piercing, but merely (merely!?) the eyes of a man who was hers if she wanted him. She put out her hand and touched his red hair and felt an overmastering urge to take him to bed.

"Oh, Dave," she said. "I have so much work to do."

"What are you telling me?"

"You're so sweet. I'm enormously attracted to you. But it isn't a good time to do this. Not in my life, not even in the liturgical calendar."

"Is that a no?"

"Yes, it's a no."

He sighed. "Will you sleep with me, then?"

It would be very good. "Not right now."

"Okay." He started the car again. "A bad time in the liturgical calendar. Well, what would be good? How about St. Swithin's Day?"

"When is that?"

"Day after tomorrow." He pulled into traffic.

She laughed. "No, Dave. But I'll tell you what. If we're both still interested and we're both still here, we'll get together on the feast day of Saint Hilda of Whitby."

"And when is that?"

"I don't know. I'll have to look it up."

"What do you mean, if we're both still here? Are you thinking of going away?"

"Not willingly, but the diocese wants to close my church."

"When?"

"I don't know. Imminently. The Archdeacon is supposed to meet me after church today. He might be there right now, all stiff stark alone with my last remaining two parishioners."

"Can I come to church? That will make three."

"You're so sweet." She sighed. "Yes, please come. I can use all the support I can get."

High Street was starting to look really terrible, with two burned-out hulks of buildings staring at each other across the way. Mother Grey wondered if there was anything at all left of the Weaver in the charred ruin of the rectory, perhaps a scrap of wood, or the scroll, that she could keep for a memento. Later that day, she would search through the rubble.

Strangely, there was no place to park in front of the church. Dave dropped her off and went to park his car around the corner. She was expecting Ralph and Mrs. van Buskirk to be waiting on the steps for her to let them in, but no one was outside the church at all.

Then she remembered she had given Saraleigh the keys. Ralph must have got them from her and let himself in. With luck he would be all set up, maybe the furnace would even be running this one last time. She went in by the side door that led into the working sacristy and began to get into her vestments. Something was strange.

Something was very strange. The furnace was indeed running, but there were unusual smells, and a warmth in the place that went beyond furnace warmth. Furthermore, there was a quality of the sound, a murmuring, and yet a deadness, almost as if many people in their winter coats were making noises and then immediately absorbing all the echoes. Almost as if St. Bede's were entirely full.

She went out into the chancel and found that it was true.

Saraleigh and her children were there. She must have passed Mother Grey and Dave Dogg on the road somehow between here and the hospital. All the boys from Ralph's group home were there. Hester Winkle and Ida Mae Soames were there from the nursing home. The Wellworths had come back with their little baby, in spite of everything. Jack Kreevitch was there with his wife and five children. But didn't they go to the Roman church? She knew Horace Burkhardt did, and there he sat next to Delight van Buskirk. Chief Harry and the rest of the police force were there with their wives and children. Delight van Buskirk's grandchildren were there. Sheila and Jake had come too, Sheila in her furs.

The homeless from the Hotel Ford sat in the back, reeking of last night's whiskey and the many days that had passed since their last baths. There were children with them too. Every pew was filled, every face wreathed in smiles. The sight nearly stopped her heart.

And there on the aisle in the fourth row was the Archdeacon. He wore a peculiar look on his face, as if he knew that someone was playing a rude joke on him but he hadn't yet figured out who, or what the point was.

There was only one thing to be said: "Morning Prayer will be found on page forty-two of the Prayer Book." If they did Morning Prayer instead of Holy Eucharist, no one would have to come up to the altar rail and take Communion. Roman Catholics weren't supposed to do that in an Episcopal Church, and Jews wouldn't do it at all. Archdeacon Megrim would surely notice the large numbers of the congregation who remained in their seats.

"O Lord, open thou our lips."

"And our mouth shall show forth thy praise," they all responded, just as though they did it every Sunday. Mother Grey led them through the entire service of Morning Prayer, not forgetting to pray for the soul of poor Phyllis, and they followed along with perfect aplomb, even the homeless. Ralph read the lessons.

When it was over, she stood at the front portal and shook everyone's hand. They said, "How nice to see you." "Good morning, Mother Vinnie. What an inspiring sermon." Had she preached a sermon? The Lord must have had control of her lips; she couldn't remember saying anything. "Good morning, Mother Grey. It's nice to be here."

It was the happiest day of her life.

On his way out Horace Burkhardt gave her a broad wink and put something into her hand. It crackled. Money? A check? She tucked it in her sleeve. Dave and Freddy were near the end of the line of people. "Saraleigh tells me she and the other vestry members have some business with you and the Archdemon after church," Dave said. "I thought I'd just take Fred here and go out for ice cream. See you later."

"Oh, boy! Ice cream!" said Fred. When they had all gone away, the townspeople leaving an overflowing collection plate, the homeless leaving only the rich and strange air where they had been,

Mother Grey drew out the paper from Horace and took a peek at it. It was a note.

The house on the north side of St. Bede's is one of mine, it said. *You can stay there rent-free for three months. After that I can't afford the taxes. Or you can have it for $100,000. The key is over the lintel.*

It was signed *Horace*.

She turned around and there in the narthex stood the Archdeacon, annoyed and bewildered, glancing at his watch, with a folder of papers under his arm. Crowded around him, all grinning like idiots, were Delight van Buskirk, Ralph, Saraleigh, and Martine and Albert Wellworth. The young mothers carried their babies.

"Good morning, Mother Grey," said Archdeacon Megrim.

"Good morning," she said.

"Ain't you gonna introduce us vestry members to Archie here?" said Saraleigh.

"Oh . . . oh, of course. Forgive me. Father Megrim, may I present Saraleigh Kane and Martine and Albert Wellworth. Little Henry Wellworth was baptized here last week. Of course you've met Mrs. van Buskirk, and Ralph." She was babbling. Vestry members? But she hadn't sworn them in. "Could you excuse us for a moment, Father? I need to speak with Saraleigh and the Wellworths." She drew them away, into the other corner of the narthex.

"How happy I am to see you," she said.

"We told you we'd be back, Mother Grey," said Albert Wellworth.

"I'm sorry," she said. "It's just that everything was so awful last week that I assumed . . ."

"Grandmom Wellworth told me I should get a real church," said his wife, "but, I don't know, St. Bede's seems real enough to me."

"A happ'nin' place," agreed Saraleigh. "Is it okay for us to be on your vestry?"

"It's wonderful," said Mother Grey. "But shush. I have to swear you in." The babies were beginning to stir and make noise. Trying to sound conversational for the Archdeacon's sake, she remarked in a chatty tone, "You have been called to a ministry in this congregation. Will you, as long as you are engaged in this work, perform it with diligence?"

"We will," they said.

"Will you faithfully and reverently execute the duties of your ministry to the honor of God, and the benefit of the members of this congregation?"

"We will, we will."

"In the name of God and of this congregation, I commission you as Members of the Vestry in the parish of St. Bede's."

"Amen," they all said. "Let's go get 'im," added Saraleigh.

The Archdeacon was glancing at his watch again, while Delight van Buskirk bent his ear about the excellent Father Bingley. "I've known him since he was a little boy," she said. "I went to school with his mother."

"What a pity that Father Bingley couldn't have been with us today. He would have found it . . .

enlightening," said the Archdeacon. He glanced around. The old church looked particularly charming this morning, with the sun's rays slanting through the dust motes and the windows twinkling.

"Yes, it's a shame," agreed Mother Grey. "But then, he had his own services to hold at St. Dinarius. Now, what can we do for you today, Father?"

The Archdeacon sighed a long sigh. "Mother Grey," he said, "I came here to urge you and the members of your vestry to accept the offer from St. Dinarius to merge St. Bede's with their parish." He opened the folder and took out a check, *Pay to the order of St. Bede's, Remarkable Fire and Casualty Company.* "Clearly the rectory was underinsured. You'll never rebuild it for a hundred and fifty thousand."

A hundred and fifty thousand? "I brought with me a release for you to sign," he said, "so that we could turn this money over to the diocese to do God's work, Mother Grey, and leave you free to accept a call from some other parish."

A hundred and fifty thousand dollars. St. Bede's could buy Horace's house, and with the other fifty thousand or whatever was left after closing costs and taxes, she could shelter the homeless, feed the hungry, even buy a ticket to Washington and lobby for government help. How big was that house of Horace's, anyway? Did it have much of a backyard? She had never noticed the place. If there was a yard, she could open a day care center here in town. A few children, a small staff. Women like Saraleigh could go out and get work, make decent lives for themselves.

"With all due respect, Father," said Mother Grey, "I believe we can do God's work with that money right here." She put out her hand for the check, which he withdrew.

Mrs. van Buskirk plucked him by the sleeve. "Dear Father Bingley is very nice," she said, "but Mother Grey is our pastor. She has done wonderful work here at St. Bede's. The things she has started, just in the few months she's been here—programs for old people, support groups for alcoholics and battered women—"

"I dunno where I'd be without Mother Vinnie," said Ralph. "Dead, probably. I used to try to kill myself."

Surprised and pleased, Mother Grey thought, "Why yes, I did do that, didn't I?" Truly the grace of God was empowering. Of course it was ridiculous about Ralph; he never really meant to kill himself.

"Mother Grey has a lot of stuff to do here. Maybe a wedding, huh, Ralphie?" Saraleigh winked at Ralph and took his arm.

"You can see for yourself she has more than doubled the congregation," said Albert Wellworth.

"I can see for myself," said the Archdeacon, "that Mother Grey's ministry here is far more vital than I had supposed it to be."

But as he took out the check again, Mother Grey's conscience suddenly smote her. *I've just done a terrible thing. I said an entire Morning Prayer service for personal gain, to mislead the Archdeacon.* He thought all those people were her new parishioners. "Father," she said, "I don't want to deceive you any longer. Most of the people who were here this morning aren't regular communicants at St. Bede's." On the other hand, she really had more than doubled the congregation. Two times three is six, and if you counted the babies . . .

"I know they aren't your parishioners, Mother Grey. But they're people of the town who feel that you and St. Bede's have an important contribution to make in Fishersville. Or am I not correct in this assumption? They weren't hired to come here, were they?"

"No, Father," she said, with a glance at the flowing alms basin. "Quite the the contrary."

"By the way, as long as we're on the subject, this *is* your real vestry, isn't it?"

"Oh, yes," she said.

"I do have one concern. If you stay here, where are you going to live?"

She handed him Horace's note.

He gave her the note back, together with the check. "Then this check is for you and the vestry of St. Bede's, Mother," he said. "Don't forget that you'll need some of this money to bulldoze the old rectory."

"I'll keep it in mind."

"It was very nice to meet you all. Now, if you'll excuse me, I must go and explain the situation here to certain members of the Department of Missions."

He left. They all cheered and hugged each other. "Did Horace Burkhardt tell you about the house?" Saraleigh asked her.

"He gave me a note," she said, wondering if there might not be some tactful way to get Saraleigh to stop chewing gum in church. "He said the key was over the lintel. Why don't we go look at it?" A day care center. There were latchkey kids all over Fishersville who would certainly benefit. She could hire a bus and take them on field trips to the Franklin Institute in Philadelphia. She could give courses in remedial reading. She could teach them to play the cello. It would be days before she thought to ask herself how Saraleigh knew about the house, or why all those people had happened to be in church this morning.

In the back row someone had carelessly left the Book of Common Prayer on the seat. She picked it up to put it where it belonged, in the rack on the back of the pew in front, and almost by accident it fell open in her hand to the Calendar of the Church Year. Hilda, Abbess of Whitby, 680. November 18. *My word, that's next week.*

Then again, she didn't have to mention it to Dave.